Take No More

SEB KIRBY
TAKE NO MORE

CANELO

First published in the United Kingdom in 2010 by Seb Kirby

This edition published in the United Kingdom in 2020 by

Canelo Digital Publishing Limited
Third Floor, 20 Mortimer Street
London W1T 3JW
United Kingdom

A CIP catalogue record for this book is available from the British Library.

Print ISBN 978 1 78863 933 0
Ebook ISBN 978 1 78863 653 7

Look for more great books at www.canelo.co

Printed and bound in Great Britain by Clays Ltd, Elcograf S.p.A.

Part One

London
Friday August 29ᵗʰ to Sunday August 31ˢᵗ

Chapter 1

I could not have known that this day, of all days, was the one that would change my life so much for the worse.

I was walking down the steps at the side of Southwark Cathedral. I'd left work in time to get to Borough Market while it was still open. Julia was away in Florence working on a project for her conservation studio, absorbed in her work restoring paintings and we hadn't seen each other for over a month.

The old Market had been transformed in recent years with the arrival from all over the world of so many young workers in London. Now almost every taste and every cuisine was catered for at the bustling stalls wedged beneath the Victorian overhead railway, its cast iron supports forming an ornate roof.

It was still a wonder to me how much I loved Julia. And how much she loved me. We were soul mates. It was as simple as that. Nor could I believe how lucky we'd been to buy the apartment overlooking the Thames.

As I left the Market, the view across the river, taking in the Embankment and with St Paul's dominating the opposite skyline, was magnificent. The Thames was always in flow, turbulent and full of interest, a working river with craft of all shapes and sizes.

Turning onto the riverside walk, popular with tourists but still retaining enough of the character that for centuries had made it a mysterious place, I walked on through a low brick walled tunnel where a busker, no doubt a young musician from one of the London orchestras, was playing Brahms. I walked past the terrace restaurant at the base of our apartment building, typed in the security number on the touchpad, pushed open the door and walked up the flight of stairs that led to the apartment.

Something was wrong. The door to the apartment was open; not ajar, but open just four or five inches.

We never left the door open no matter how good the security system of the apartment building was supposed to be.

I approached the door, trembling. I pushed against it. It would hardly give; there was something behind the door, stopping it from opening. I pushed harder until it gave. I forced my way inside.

It was Julia. She'd collapsed against the inside of the door trying to escape the apartment. There was blood everywhere.

I felt for a pulse – at her wrist, at her neck – but there was none.

I felt the deepest sadness welling from the base of my soul. It began with a scream that progressed to a howl of bitter regret followed by tears that shook my whole body.

Someone had killed her. Her body was still warm. It must have happened not many minutes before.

Chapter 2

The police arrived quickly after my call.

I hadn't been allowed to remain in the apartment for long. While a forensic team set to work analysing the scene, it was politely suggested it would be better if I gave as much information as possible at the station to allow them to track the killer.

The inspector – his name was Hendricks – had been very persuasive.

I'd been with a female police officer in a small room in Euston police station for over an hour, nominally receiving grief counselling. But there was something false about her manner, as if she was stalling while elsewhere in the building enquiries were being made – about what I did not know.

And now I was sitting on an uncomfortable chair in an adjacent interview room that smelt of sweat and corruption, answering questions. I'd been through the immediate events: Name – James Blake. Age – thirty-one. Occupation – radio producer. Height – 6' 1". Eyes – hazel green.

Where had I been that day? Why had I returned to the apartment? How I had found Julia? Why had I not expected her return?

Nothing I said was flagged up as out of place.

"Mr Blake, can you think of any reason why your wife should have been killed?"

Hendricks, who shaved his head on the assumption that no one would then notice his pattern baldness, had eyes that were slightly far apart. There was a look in those eyes that told me if we were the last two people alive I would not have wanted to trust him.

My mind was not functioning. The shock had been too great.

Why would anyone want to kill her? It made no sense.

"Can you think of any threats made to her? Any enemies?" Hendricks continued.

"No, nothing, I mean... no one." It was all I could bring myself to say.

What was the point? She was gone. That was the inescapable, saddest fact.

"Your wife; it's almost certain she knew her attacker," Hendricks said. "There was no forced entry, either at the main entrance to the apartments or at your door."

Eighty per cent of murders are carried out by persons known to the victim. So, was it any surprise the police often looked as close to home as possible?

"I just can't imagine anyone who would want to do harm to Julia."

"We'll just have to follow up on all her contacts," Hendricks said with an underlying note of resignation. "If you can't help, that is." Why did it feel they were already thinking of fitting me up? Whatever happened to the grief counselling?

What did they know that they were not telling me? How did they think I would be able to help them when I was so distressed?

"She kept an address book in her bedside drawer."

"We have it." Hendricks looked disappointed. "It will take quite some time to work our way through that list. And we have the computer from the apartment. We've taken it away for examination. Your computer?"

"Yes, that's mine. Julia uses a laptop."

"Which is where?"

"At her work. At the conservation studio."

"So there's nothing unusual you know of about your wife's recent contacts?"

"I don't know what you expect me to tell you."

"You could begin by telling me about your wife's affair."

There was no compassion in Hendricks' voice.

Chapter 3

I didn't want to think about it.

Someone had told me, I couldn't quite remember who it was. It could have been my brother Miles who had been working as a journalist for over ten years now. The police know how to lie to get a result.

Why else would Hendricks be saying Julia had been unfaithful? Was it no more than a trick to help them to pin Julia's murder on me?

Or had they found something in Julia's possessions in the hour they'd kept me waiting?

"I have no idea what you mean," I said. My thoughts were beginning to clear enough for me to face up to what the inspector had told me.

"Your wife, Mr Blake, she was an attractive woman." Hendricks was warming to the task. "She spent time away in her work; she must have been hit on by any number of men trying their luck. You don't think she would not have finally given in to the charms of one of the Italian gigolos she was bound to have met on her art conservation travels?" He almost made *art conservation* sound like a perversion. "Florence, wasn't it?"

I could feel my anger rising. It was emerging despite the weight of the grief I felt. Hendricks was deliberately playing with my fears. Hoping to get lucky, hoping I would break down and, if there had been an affair, he could develop this as a motive.

"Look, my wife has been killed, I'm in a state of shock, and you're making insinuations she was being unfaithful. Tell me what you know. Or leave me alone."

"I know what you must be feeling." There was a note of compassion in the inspector's voice that I didn't buy. "But you know we have to get at the facts as quickly as possible. We found this."

Hendricks passed across the table a postcard sealed in a transparent evidence bag. It was a typical tourist scene, showing the Ponte Vecchio in Florence resplendent at night, straddling the Arno.

"Turn it over."

I read the words in the message with growing fear and anguish. The message said:

> *As ever, my perfect love.*
> *Remember Michelangelo's slaves.*
> *I can't wait to see you again.*
> Giancarlo

"We found it near her bedside table, between the pages in the book she'd been reading. Do you know this Giancarlo?" Hendricks asked. "Go on, tell me. He's been poking her all the time she was out in Florence and you got to know all about it and you came up with the idea of having her killed and walking away with the deeds to that nice flat overlooking the Thames, didn't you?"

"You must be crazy."

"We checked. The insurance on the apartment was increased only six weeks ago. If either of you died, the other would pick up enough to pay off the mortgage. A cool half million."

"Our solicitor told us to do it. The value of the apartment has almost doubled since we bought it. You know what London property prices are like. There is nothing sinister in that and I don't know who the hell Giancarlo is or why he would be writing to my wife like that. And I didn't kill her."

"She's back in London and she doesn't phone you or text you?"

"I haven't heard from her."

"It's funny," Hendricks said, "we haven't been able to find her phone. How many women get separated from their phones? On your own account, she's made a sudden change of plan and yet doesn't try to contact you. Why would she do that?"

"I don't know why… I'm struggling to understand any of this."

"Her lover. Giancarlo. It's not that deep is it?" Hendricks paused. "It's the sort of thing that could lead to subterfuge and, if you knew about it, the sort of thing that could arouse a certain jealousy of mind. Enough to have your wife killed."

"What makes you think it was someone who had planned to have her killed? It could have been a failed burglary, some demented crack-head trying to steal enough for the next fix."

"I don't think so," Hendricks said. "We haven't had the full autopsy report back yet but the pathologist has seen cases like this before. He phoned straight away as soon as he saw the pattern of the damage to your wife's head."

There was worse to come. Hendricks was playing with me.

"The bullet had been expertly tampered with. The killer used a dum–dum to make sure the slug didn't pass through your wife's head but expanded at the base of her brain when she was shot in the back of the head."

Hendricks paused.

"Mr Blake, whoever did this intended to kill."

"So you think I hired someone to kill my own wife and then went to the apartment to find her dying in my arms?"

"You tell me, Mr Blake. The one thing you learn in this line of work is there is no end to the devious intentions of our fellow man. People think it throws people like me off the scent. They couldn't be more wrong."

Chapter 4

I was allowed one call. My brother, Miles, was in London, staying at the Bridge Hotel close to London Bridge Station. We'd met for lunch the day before. I placed the call.

Within an hour I was out. The solicitor Miles had brought with him must have known his craft well. Hendricks was left with no reason to hold me, though he made it clear he did not approve of the release.

Even so, I had my fingerprints taken and I had to give a nasal swab so my DNA could be analysed and logged. The result would remain on the police database no matter what the outcome of their investigation. It was not enough that I'd been brought to the station and questioned. No doubt they would be trying all they could to match my DNA to what they'd found at the crime scene.

"I want you to report here every day," Hendricks had said.

"Does that mean I'm a suspect?"

"Let's just say we will need to talk to you again at short notice and you should not stray too far. Make sure you give us the address where you're staying before you leave."

I couldn't go back to the apartment; even if I could have faced that, it would be off-limits for some days while the police continued their investigation. Miles suggested

I should stay at his hotel and within half an hour of being released we were sitting in Miles' room. It was more of a suite with a large seating area and more than a hint of comfort about it.

Miles had noted my expression. "It's on expenses. The newspaper picks up the tab when I have to work in London. It's a major that should lead to a story with worldwide importance." But then, remembering the gravity of the situation, his voice lowered. "I can't tell you how sorry I am."

"They've killed her," I said. "I don't know how I'm going to come to terms with that. But I'll tell you something, whoever they are, whoever did this thing, I'm going to find them and I'm going to make sure they get the justice they deserve."

"Jim, you don't know who they are, where they came from, why they killed her, what kind of people you might be dealing with."

"So, help me, Miles."

This was just the opposite of how it was when we were kids, growing up in Birmingham. I was the elder brother, Miles the youngster, looking up to his big brother, James, who just by virtue of being three years older had been made to be the responsible one. Only now it was big brother saying never mind about caution, fight back whatever the risk.

"Of course, I'll do everything I can to help you, Jim."

"I've got to do this for Julia." I could barely hold back the tears. "It's the only thing that makes sense."

I didn't doubt my brother knew I was serious. We had shared a difficult and precarious childhood. The family had been poor even by the lowered standards of the

14

Birmingham families around us. Our father, Danny, was some kind of war hero. He'd fought in the Falklands war back in 1982, yomping into Port Stanley, striking the fear of God into those ill-prepared conscripts in the Argentinian army. No doubt, he'd killed. But like all those who killed in war he'd chosen not to talk about it.

Our mother, June, had tried her best to present us as a normal family but the marriage never recovered when Danny came home from the war. There were fights, endless arguments, and the children, James and Miles, would frequently get drawn in. There was invariably some petty pretext, some minor crime of which me or Miles were supposedly guilty. The more our mother sought to defend us, the more Danny took this as a sign that his wife was turning his children against him. It became one of those vicious spirals where the next inevitable incident fed off the embers of the last.

And violence, real violence, broke out when things got really twisted and began running out of control.

As the elder child, I always chose to put myself in the firing line, protecting my mother, protecting my younger brother. It had hardened me. Facing down limitless rage, not knowing when the threat of violence might break in again, had made me ever on my guard, ever careful to try to head off the next incident.

And being the eldest, I'd become a confidante to my mother. When my father was at work, she would offload her troubles, seek my advice, tell me about their failed sex life, tell me how difficult it was to keep the family together. So by the age of twelve, I'd become wise, too wise, in the ways of the world.

Danny was not a bad man. He was the victim of circumstance. I came to realise that as I grew older. But it hadn't made my childhood an easy one.

The escape had been through education. By burying myself in schoolwork I could block out the seemingly endless problems that surrounded me. I had a flair for mathematics that developed into an interest in science. I passed the exams. I wanted to succeed.

But I learned early on that aggression would get me nowhere. I'd been provoked by a kid in school who deserved to be taken down a peg. And, hardened as I was, when it had come down to it, I found it easy to overcome him and hurt him. Somehow I'd broken a golden rule. The schoolyard violence was meant to be symbolic, with no one really getting hurt. And I'd hurt that kid for real and it had shocked everyone. I'd been in big trouble and was almost expelled. But in the end I escaped with the sternest warning, and I'd learned that if I wanted to succeed I would have to believe violence got you nowhere and reason and tolerance and understanding the other's point of view was what mattered.

And I'd lived that way for the past twenty of my thirty-one years. It had been a success – I'd gone to university, I'd won a good physics degree. I'd become a successful radio producer and had joined the ranks of the good and would-be great.

And now those bastards had killed Julia, without a second thought. That had thrown everything into doubt.

"Try to concentrate on the facts," Miles said. "Have you checked your messages? Perhaps Julia tried to contact you?"

I took out my phone, slipped it out of its case and pressed the scroll wheel. There were about twenty email messages waiting. The usual rubbish about changing the security code at banks I'd never been with, offers from Nigerian inheritors of oil fortunes who needed just a small investment to free up ten million dollars and all those messages from all those companies I'd made one time contact with who now had me on their list.

And right in the middle of all the dross was a message posted earlier that day from Julia. I hadn't seen it until now.

I clicked to open the message.

Her last message: *help me.*

There was an attachment. I clicked on its icon and the data began to download from the server.

As I waited I felt that at least this link remained with Julia, however slight, however tenuous.

The screen filled up as the download was completed. It was just a single picture.

I gave it to Miles who frowned as he looked at it.

It showed a naked woman cradling between her legs the head of a large swan. The woman was corpulent, as beautiful women were supposed to be in classical times. The swan's long neck was supremely phallic. It was very sensual, very erotic.

"What on earth is that?"

Miles allowed himself a smile. "It's *Leda and the Swan,*" he said in a knowing tone. "The guy I palled up with at university, Charles Dowd, he was a big Bjork fan. Had posters of all her album covers on the walls of his room. You had to notice the one where the photo of Bjork is overlaid with a traced outline of a swan. He was into all sorts of stuff about his favourite singer. Told me it was a reference to the painting *Leda and the Swan*. Told me it was in the National Gallery right here in London." He paused with resumed seriousness. "So why send you an almost blank message and just that picture?"

"It's from her email address, the Hotmail one she uses from her phone and from her laptop," I said. "So it's from her. She wasn't in the habit of sending me pictures of the paintings she was working on and I don't have any idea why she would send just the picture and that message. Except she was in trouble and maybe it was the only thing she could send. I just don't know. But it's a point of connection, something about her I can still hold on to."

Miles' expression told me how sad he felt that it had come to this. "I've booked you a room just down the corridor. Get some sleep; you must be exhausted."

I spent the night without sleep, as if in a trance, seeing over and over Julia dying in my arms, then seeing the burnt-in image of the swan towering over the reclining woman. I wished it was a dream, but the truth was this was a movie loop of what I'd actually seen that would not go away.

Chapter 5

Saturday August 30th

I was not aware I was being followed until it was almost too late.

I'd set out for the National Gallery early next morning. It had been only a short walk to London Bridge station and soon I was on the descent to the underground, down the old brown walled tunnels under the oldest railway station in the city.

The weight of numbers rushing up and down the long escalators was a shock to those who were not used to such levels of crowding. To the newcomer, the senses could be easily overwhelmed, the mind led to shut down to a minimum where all but the most essential signals were ignored. But, although the passage of people around me and the distraction of the animated advertising panels was all around, I still noticed something disturbing.

The fat man in the black shirt and trousers had been behind me almost since I'd left the hotel. He was trying to look anonymous but was not succeeding. Maybe it was something about his weight and the cut of his hair. He was trying to appear natural, just another of the travellers going about their business, but there was something about his bulk that made me think he earned his living doing something altogether more physical and worrying than the average commuter.

Paranoia. Grief and pressure. Lack of sleep.

Don't be foolish.

I carried on. The fat man would soon set off on his own route. I headed down to the Jubilee Line and sought out the platform that would take me towards Charing Cross. The man was still there. I boarded the train and managed to find a seat as it set off down the tunnel. He was still there. He'd taken to standing near the exit door and was reading a free newspaper.

It couldn't be Hendricks. The police just didn't have the manpower. But if not Hendricks, then who?

I thought about challenging the man; just going up to him and taking him on right there and then. But something told me to hold back. He would just deny it and make me look like a fool.

I had to change at Waterloo. As I left the train, the man also got off and was walking along behind me, getting ever closer as we moved along the connecting passageway to the next platform.

As I rounded the end of the passageway to the new platform, I was surprised to see how empty it was. After all that crowding at London Bridge, it was difficult to understand why there were so few people here. It was part of the ebb and flow, one of the troughs in the peaks and troughs that marked the chaotic flow of humanity in one of the most crowded cities in the world.

The man was behind me, getting closer all the time. The train was about to rattle into the station. I felt there was nowhere to go. The man behind me was approaching more rapidly now; the train was just yards from the platform. It would take nothing for a man of his size to push me under the train. I had to act quickly. I stopped and turned, rushing headfirst at the bulk of the still-approaching man. The collision was painful. I felt a searing pain in my head as I made contact with his chest, but I had done enough. In the delay, the train had arrived and the doors had opened. Turning, I ran for the train, getting on well before the doors closed.

My attacker could have made it to the train but he did not try. His cover was blown. With a wry smile he pointedly dusted down his clothes, calmly walking away back down the connecting passageway.

That had not been paranoia. That had been an attempt to kill me.

I tried to control my heart rate but the adrenalin had kicked in too surely. I took deep breaths. I tried to concentrate on sharing the composure of my new fellow passengers. No one had seen a thing. I could have been pushed under this train and no one would have been any the wiser about who had done it. That was the frightening fact of the matter.

I hadn't recovered much by the time I arrived at Charing Cross. The paranoia was real. I kept looking behind me to see if the man was still there, or if he'd been replaced by another stalker. No one could be seen but that didn't make me feel any more secure.

Tell Hendricks?

What was the point? He was not going to believe me.

As I came out of the station the familiar throng of tourists that met me eased some of my fears.

Numerous children, as tradition now dictates, were clambering on the lions at the base of Nelson's column.

The pigeons, culled from their heyday, were nonetheless abundant, pecking at the corners of sandwiches tossed for them by the crowd. To my right, the reassuring sight of St Martins in the Fields peeked out from the hoardings that encased most of it in what was becoming one of the longest and most expensive of makeovers. And ahead of me, in all its kitsch classical elegance, was the National Gallery.

Entrance was free but in the event of queries by the public there was a bank of information desks to the right peopled by half a dozen receptionists. It was one of the delights of London that you could view all the art you wished for free. It was a constant dismay that ninety per cent of the visitors to the National Gallery, the Tate or Tate Modern were overseas tourists.

I didn't have long to wait. An attractive young girl with an Eastern European accent asked me what I wanted.

"I'd like to see *Leda and the Swan.*"

Despite my intentions, I must have sounded desperate. The girl became defensive immediately.

"Yes?"

"It's a painting. You have it here."

"Yes, it is in Room A." She was looking at me as though I was a problem.

"Can I see it?" I didn't know why but I was sure she was about to disappoint me.

"Only on Wednesdays," she said.

"What do you mean?" My anger was rising. "The gallery is open seven days a week."

"It's a special room. The reserve collection; we only open that room one day per week – on Wednesday afternoons."

I was not going to be able to see the picture. Wednesday was four days away. I almost lost my temper. But why take it out on this girl; she was clearly only doing her job and she must get more than her fair share of the deranged and the demented.

"Is there any way I can look at the picture?"

"You could try our intranet." Her tone was making it clear the enquiry was coming to an end. "There is a study room on the third floor. You can access the intranet there."

This was as much as I was going to get. I said thanks and headed for the study room.

I found a seat with a modem flat screen monitor and pretended to be accessing the information. But it was a long time before I began to recover even a semblance of composure.

Chapter 6

Eventually some calm returned. It was no good worrying about what had happened on the Underground. I would have to come to terms with that later. Right at this moment I needed to find some clear connection to what had happened to Julia. And the only connection I had was the picture of the painting of *Leda and the Swan* that had appeared on my phone.

So, using the National Gallery database, I searched the word 'Leda' and without delay a page came up showing the picture together with background details.

It was a sensual image. The beak of the swan was placed in the woman's mouth, its neck resting on her naked breast, the graceful curl of her right hand resting on her knee, her left hand similarly relaxed as it hung down at the side of the couch, the beatific expression on her face suggesting an almost hypnotic fulfilment. The swan's tail feathers obscured the vital parts between her open legs, as she lay prone on the couch, one leg raised to grant him access, his wings raised on either side of her as he clearly mounted her.

Yes, this was coitus, however classically portrayed.

The woman was heavy-armed and heavy-legged by today's standards but that was the way they liked them back in circa 1530 when, the accompanying blurb told me, the picture was believed to have been painted by Michelangelo.

Julia. Why such a weird picture? What were you trying to say?

The back-story was even stranger, as the attached information told me. The myth of Leda and the Swan had been around since 2000 BC or so and was recounted in Ovid's *Metamorphoses*, chronicling the actions of the gods and their interaction with mortals. Jupiter, the supreme god, also known as Zeus by the Greeks, used his power to take the shape of any animal he wanted to conceal his identity from his wife Juno as he seduced the earthly women of his choice. Leda, wife of the King of Sparta, had been visited by Jupiter as a swan. The seduction took place on the same night she'd slept with her husband Tyndareus. Jupiter had been aided by Hypnos, the goddess of sleep, who had lulled Leda with sounds of dripping water from the River Lethe and by Peitho, the goddess of persuasive seduction.

No wonder she'd been unable to resist. No wonder she had that beatific smile on her face.

If Julia had been trying to tell me something by sending me the picture, what had she meant?

And here was a reference to the poem *Leda and the Swan* by W. B. Yeats. Julia had always spoken with enthusiasm about Yeats, something to do with her Irish ancestry, I supposed.

It was time to go; there was nothing more to be gained here. I retraced my steps, back to the entrance hall, out past the receptionists and into the noise and clamour of Trafalgar Square.

Heading to the Underground, I was careful to check I was not being followed again; but there was no sign of the man in black or anyone like him. Either he'd improved his shadowing technique or the altercation earlier had put paid to the tail, at least for the time being. I found the connection to Green Park, boarded the first train, and settled into the comforting anonymity of being just another one of the passengers.

Chapter 7

It was only a short walk from Green Park station to Albemarle Street, Mayfair, where, in the area around Brown's Hotel and the numerous private art galleries that served the well heeled of London, the Clinton Ridley Restoration Studio stood. It was one of the best-known conservation studios, specialising in the preparation of sculpture and paintings for sale in the private galleries and taking in commissions from owners of art works from all around the world. This was where Julia had worked.

"Visiting?" The uniformed security man in the booth just inside the entrance was inviting me to come up with a name.

What was the name of Julia's colleague in the painting restoration department? Myra McKenzie, was that it?

I tried my luck. "Myra McKenzie, Painting Conservation." I was trying to sound as matter of fact as I could.

The security man dialled a number into his phone pad. When he got a reply, he casually looked back. "And your name?"

"James Blake." The conservators must have a continuous stream of visitors; I could be just another visitor in a busy day.

A further pause as words were exchanged over the security phone.

"Dr McKenzie will be down in a few minutes. Please take a seat." The security man gestured for me to sit on one of the hardback chairs spaced evenly along the short corridor.

When Myra McKenzie emerged through the double swing doors she seemed unsurprised to see me. "You must be Jim. I've been trying to get in touch but didn't know how to reach you. It's so awful, what happened to Julia. I'm so, so sorry. We're all in shock. Difficult to imagine how you're feeling."

I felt like breaking down there and then but I knew I had to stay strong.

She was an attractive, red-haired Scot about my age with a reassuring, maternal bearing that put people at their ease.

"Julia told me so much about you," Myra said. She was determined to move the conversation on. "About the work you do with the kids in the East End. I think it's wonderful you find time to do that when you have such a demanding job. At the radio station, isn't it?"

I didn't like to say too much about the sports club I managed at weekends, about the East End, mainly ethnic minority, kids who either had sport or crime as their life goal. Every one I won back from the streets and turned on to the dream of playing for Arsenal or West Ham or representing their country at the Olympics was one that might just have a chance of breaking out of a future that was all but determined, whether they made it in sports or not. It was about giving them confidence that things could be different and they could climb out of the hole. Just as I'd done in Birmingham a generation before when it was an easier thing to do. But it always involved more than sport. The life crises that seemed so intractable to the kids could so often be solved with a little of my own money or an appeal to a school Head who was about to expel an unruly pupil.

I said, "Can we talk?"

"Of course." Myra turned. "We can go to the lab."

I realised I could have made an appointment and Myra would have seen me. But that would have supposed I'd been paying proper attention to what had been happening in Julia's career and had access to her work contacts. Yet in my own way, I'd short-circuited the more proper approach and arrived at more or less the same place. I'd met Myra before, at one of those evenings at the conservation studio I'd attended, but not given my proper attention.

She led me along a short corridor and down a steep flight of stone steps into a basement area. It was a large studio filled with sculptures in various states of restoration, many sitting on wooden pallets that had been used to manoeuvre the pieces into place at the various work-stations using the overhead lifting gear that was dotted around at different locations. On the workbenches nearby were scattered the implements of the sculpture conser-vator's trade: everything from scalpels and chisels to spray cans and plastic boxes containing material for the making of poultices.

"This is Sculpture Conservation – the heavy end." Myra ushered me on a path through the studio that led to a further door. "It's a little more sane in here." She showed me into the Painting Restoration studio.

A young girl, an intern, was studying with great care the surface of a painting that had been positioned on an easel. Around her head she wore a device that served both

31

as a magnifier and as a means of illumination. She was paying such complete attention to a minute region on the upper left of the painting that she hadn't seen us enter.

"This is Manuela, from Madrid. She's here on placement for six months to study restoration techniques. She's working on one of a collection of Victorian paintings recently put up for sale by a client who is convinced the market has hit its peak."

The intern paused in her work, looked up and smiled from beneath the headset.

"This is James Blake."

"A pleasure," I said. I knew what Myra was doing and realised just how helpful that was. Treating me like a normal professional visitor, as just another interested party, she was offering me a slice of normality, a reassuring respite. Myra was the kind of person who demanded that those around her became more confident than they had a normal right to be.

"It's the varnish." Myra pointed to the painting. "It was fine when it was applied a hundred and fifty years ago, a good way of sealing the paint. But over the years it has discoloured, become dark brown, obscuring colours, making the painting look drab and uninteresting."

"I know what you mean," I replied. "I couldn't see anything in the Pre-Raphaelite paintings in the City Museum in my home town, Birmingham. Then one day I went again and they'd restored them, the brown, dull lifelessness had gone. There was a brightness and intensity to the colours." I recalled my discovery of Holman Hunt and Dante Gabriel Rossetti there; a key point in my release into another life.

"Exactly," Myra said. "But the trick is to remove the brown varnish without damaging the paint underneath. If the painting is worth several millions, that's quite a responsibility."

"So, we have to proceed with care," Manuela said. "With great care."

"Using a cleaning solution and cotton buds to dissolve away the varnish layer by layer, work on this single painting will take between two and three months. It's a painstaking process." Myra pointed at the corner of the painting Manuela was working on. "Which is why we've been looking for a more effective alternative – like lasers."

"Is that where Julia fits in?" I asked.

"That's right, Julia was our expert in using lasers in the restoration of paintings."

So strange and sad to hear Julia talked about in the past tense.

"I guess the laser can do what the liquid is doing, only better?"

"Yes, it can remove material one layer at a time, it's more controllable. And we use lasers in other ways, for viewing the kind of conservation work required, finding the defects that need repair. That was Julia's real expertise, she used lasers and techniques like terahertz imaging to investigate the condition of a painting."

"I should have been more involved in what she was doing. I didn't know what she was working with."

"It's a technique she'd become more interested in during the past two or three years. You might say, it had become a major taking off point in her career."

All that time together with Julia, so little time spent on what was of real interest to her.

"Terahertz imaging lets you look inside the painting surface," Myra continued. "If you couple it with one of the computer profiling programs that are available, you can make a map, starting at the surface, going down layer by layer, one map for each layer until you get right down to the canvas. We use it to find out where the problems are. And of course, if the artist has made any preliminary markings on the canvas before starting to paint, you can see those too."

I said, "You would get an idea of how the artist planned the picture?"

"Yes, in some cases you can see outlines of whole underpaintings too. Sometimes it's the artist's method of working, building up the image from a series of painted layers, but occasionally it is something quite different. Sometimes someone else has painted a whole new image on top of an older image. Terahertz lets you see the outline of the painting underneath: we're starting to discover that the existence of underpaintings is more common than people thought."

"And Julia was interested in underpaintings?"

"Of course! She was determined to discover missing masterpieces that had been thought to be lost. She was convinced many had in fact been overpainted rather than destroyed and built up a hit list of masterpieces that in her terms were waiting to be discovered."

"Why paint over a masterpiece?"

"You have to remember," Myra said, "the artists we consider great today weren't all thought of that way just a few years ago. If you go back fifty years Caravaggio was little admired. Shakespeare's tragedies weren't much appreciated until recent times. Each age selects its own geniuses from the past to suit its own needs. It's always been that way."

"So someone looks at the frame and the prepared canvas and thinks they will use those for their own painting, without any way of realising that from the point of view of a future time they will have been painting over a masterpiece?"

"That's about it. Or sometimes a painting condemned as being immoral or blasphemous might be saved from being destroyed. No one would have been sure back then how to recover it at a later date but a masterpiece may have been spared by having been concealed in that way."

I took out my phone and opened the attachment on the e-mail from Julia. I showed the image to Myra whose eyes opened wide in recognition.

"*Leda and the Swan!*" She recognised it without hesitation. "That was one of Julia's targets. It was on her list of lost paintings she was trying to rediscover."

"It's in the National Gallery," I said. "I went over to see it earlier but it seems almost no one is allowed to get near it."

"But you know the National Gallery painting is a copy, don't you, Jim? It was donated by the Duke of Northumberland in 1838. The original by Michelangelo was a commission by the Duke of Ferrara sometime around 1530. But somehow the painting ended up being delivered to the King of France. It's one of the greatest of the masterpieces known to be missing. The official line is that it was eventually deliberately destroyed as immoral but perhaps it was just plain lost; no one knows. Julia was convinced there was a fair chance that paintings like this had been overpainted and she would find an original Michelangelo by using her terahertz technique. I would say it was in her Top Ten. But where did you get the image?"

"It's the last thing Julia sent me before she died," I said. "She attached it to the e-mail she sent before she was killed."

Myra's look told me everything I needed to know about her anguish at the loss of a colleague who was also a good friend. Despite the reassurance she was giving me, I was convinced she must be on the point of tears.

Chapter 8

We retreated to what had been Julia's office on the far side of the Painting Conservation studio, leaving Manuela to her work. Myra had made it clear with a mere movement of eyes that we should talk somewhere with more privacy.

"I'd like to see Julia's computer," I said.

"The police inspector..." she began.

"Hendricks," I reminded her.

"Yes, Inspector Hendricks, he was here earlier today and insisted on taking it with him as evidence."

I couldn't hide my disappointment. Getting access to Julia's computer was my main strategy of beginning to find out what had happened. Hendricks was in my way.

"Did she make a backup?"

"As a matter of fact, she did. Not that Hendricks asked. I might have told him but since he didn't consider it, I thought that might be something you would be interested in. That's why I was pleased to see you here."

She took out a small key from the top left hand drawer of Julia's desk, used it to unlock the adjacent filing cabinet, reached inside and removed a pocket drive. She handed it to me. "Doesn't look like much, but this little baby holds 180 gigabytes. I placed it in the drawer before Hendricks arrived."

"She backed everything up?"

"Of course. Everyone should do it, but how many of us do? But just over a year ago, Julia started doing this with everything that came in to her computer – e-mails, attachments, Word files, you name it."

"She didn't say what had changed?"

"I didn't ask her. I assumed it must be something to do with the need for security when dealing with her contacts or to do with internal politics here. But she never gave me any details; I wasn't expected to pry and I never did. Now after what's happened, I wish I had."

"So, Hendricks has all the information from Julia's computer?"

"Not exactly. He phoned a few hours after they'd taken her computer away. He was quite indignant, implying Julia must have been some sort of terrorist or drugs runner. She'd encrypted all of the files."

"And that means the backup files on the pocket drive are also likely to be encrypted." I weighed the small device on the palm of my hand.

"I'm afraid so," Myra said. "256-bit encryption comes as standard on half a dozen shareware programs that just run straight from your desktop. Without the password, you have to work your way through a few trillion alternatives to get to open the files by chance."

"I suppose we don't know Julia's password. She wouldn't have written it down or kept it in a non-encrypted file in case she forgot it?"

"It's just not like her. If it was meant to be secret, Julia would have been very good at doing just that, I'm sure you know that."

Myra was right. Julia would not have made such a mistake. I could feel the hope of getting near to her again in some intangible way through the files she'd copied to the pocket drive melting away. I knew what Hendricks would be saying. She was keeping things secret to conceal her affair with Giancarlo and whatever she was up to in Florence. I knew I had to clear such doubts from my mind.

I slipped the portable drive into my jacket pocket. "Thanks."

I had to find the password. I knew so much about how Julia's mind worked that I had a much better chance than Hendricks of finding out what the files held.

"Don't let Hendricks know I have the backup drive. If he knows I have it, he's bound to sequester it as evidence."

"Of course," Myra said. "And if I can help in any way, just ask."

I thanked her again as she escorted me back to the exit at the security desk. I made my way to Tottenham Court Road station, checking all the way for any sign of a tail, but there appeared to be none. I took the train to Bank, made the short walk to my office at the radio station and logged in from my workplace laptop computer. After sending an e-mail message to my boss, saying I would need to take time off on compassionate leave, and emailing my co-manager, Rui, to let him know I would not be able to make football practice for a while, I withdrew a slipcase from the desk drawer, placed the laptop and Julia's drive in it, tucked it under my arm and walked out of the building, nodding farewell to the security guard.

I called at the booth of the left luggage company at Charing Cross station, paid the fee and left the computer and the drive for safekeeping.

Chapter 9

When I arrived back at the hotel, Hendricks was waiting in the lobby.

"You've been less than responsible," he said. "You should have reported to the station by now."

My head was swimming. I wanted to go to the room; I needed room service and sleep and rest. I didn't want to have to talk to Hendricks.

"So you just came by on the off chance I suppose." I sat on the couch facing the inspector. "Or have you been getting someone to follow me all day?"

"Let's say we've been concerned about you but don't have the manpower."

"You didn't see a big guy dressed in black try to push me under a train, did you?"

Hendricks looked anything but alarmed or puzzled. "You're under some strain, you say?"

"I thought it was your job to investigate crime. Or do you just sit in the station and wait on the DNA evidence to implicate someone?"

"Your wife's computer," Hendricks said. "The one at her work. Did you know all the files on it have been encrypted, not with anything simple – strong encryption, 256-bit?"

"I had no idea." I tried to make sure I sounded noncommittal. "What she did at work was her own affair."

"You don't know your wife's password, I suppose?"

"Now, if I was unaware Julia was using encryption, how would I know she had a password?" It hadn't been a very well laid trap.

"There you go again," Hendricks said with a note of feigned desperation. "Answering my question with a question."

"I don't know of any password my wife may have had for any files she may have encrypted."

"Well, we've got a team of security consultants working on this. They'll get there, and sooner or later we will know just what your wife had taken so much trouble to conceal."

There was something else. Hendricks was just waiting for his moment.

"We needed a formal identification of your wife's body. You haven't reported at the station as you said you would. So we contacted your wife's parents and your brother and they came in for the identification. They've done that now, so we won't need to ask you to do it. In any case, we'd matched your wife's DNA to the hair sample we'd found on a brush close to her bed. But you weren't available."

"I was out all day."

"Not answering your phone."

"There are some places where you have to turn your phone off."

"Anywhere you like to tell us about?"

"Nowhere important, really. At the National Gallery looking at paintings."

Hendricks raised an eyebrow. "Anyway, I need to ask you to sign this." He pushed a one-page form in front of me. It was a consent form for Julia's body.

I'd forgotten about all that. I should have been contacting Julia's family, telling them the terrible news, making plans for her funeral. Hendricks said Miles was doing it.

But there was something else. Hendricks knew when to come to the hotel. I'd turned the phone on again when I left the conservation studio, and they must have been using it to track me.

"What are you asking me to sign?"

"It's just a formality. We're going to have to keep your wife's body for some time to check we haven't missed anything."

"Are you talking days or weeks?"

"I'd say weeks, Mr Blake. We've had the first run of evidence and analysis back from the lab. Guess what – we found your DNA all over your wife's body."

"I found her. I tried to revive her. When I saw she was dead, I cradled her in my arms and wept. You might expect to find some DNA."

"Exactly."

"That supposed killer you mentioned; he would have known enough not to leave a trace…" I realised almost as soon as I said it I was being led into an area of dialogue I should avoid.

"Why don't you tell me about him, Mr Blake?"

"You should know better than that, Inspector."

It was Miles. He'd returned to the hotel and had made a beeline for the corner of the lobby where Hendricks and I were sitting.

"Time was when the police gave a formal warning if there was any chance a potential suspect might be led to make incriminating comments." Miles looked suitably stern and informed.

"It's not important anyway." Hendricks knew he'd been thwarted.

I signed the form that consigned Julia's body to police possession.

"Come on, Hendricks," Miles said, "can't you see he's tired, distressed? Cut him some slack."

Hendricks could see he would get no further and appeared to be relieved when his phone rang and he could make excuses to leave.

"Not the world's greatest humanitarian," Miles observed. "Jim, you need to start looking after yourself. When did you last eat a proper meal?"

"I was going to get something brought up to the room."

"That just won't do. I booked a table in the hotel restaurant for tonight. I expect you to join me there, after you've had some rest."

I could see what Miles was up to – being the supportive brother. But of course he was right. No point letting myself go.

By the time I'd been up to the room, showered, shaved, and put on a change of clothes, I'd regained enough composure to realise the only way I was going to find the truth about Julia was to make sure I didn't allow myself to get this low again. I lay on the bed and dreamed of our time together – the sunlight in her hair, the smell of her when she emerged from the shower, the touch of her gentle fingers caressing my shoulders and back; things you can only recall with your eyes closed.

When I woke, I realised the afternoon was gone and I was late for the meal with Miles.

The dinner was good. Served in a mock colonial Indian dining room. I needed the food, but I also needed the steady company of Miles who was adept at steering the conversation away from the immediate trauma. But inevitably, I felt compelled to return to the facts that were troubling me.

"I found out about the picture," I said. "The one Julia sent to my phone. You were right about *Leda and the Swan*."

Miles looked down. "Have you discovered anything more about why Julia sent it?"

"I don't know much more, Miles. I don't know how she's ended up dead and why she would send me that picture. But it's the only thing I've got."

I told Miles about the visit to Clinton Ridley Conservation studio and about Julia's encrypted pocket drive.

"There could be something there," Miles said. "Just tell me what I can do to help."

"Julia's parents, did you speak to them? I just couldn't face them right now."

"After they came to see her, to make the identification, they were very distressed, as you would expect."

I'd always found it difficult to get on with Julia's parents. It was more than the usual barrier you would expect when a daughter so dear to them had set off on her own path in life with a man they would not have chosen for her. No, there was something else there that I couldn't understand.

45

"I'll try to meet up with them tomorrow," I said. In fact, I knew this was something I would avoid.

We talked on almost until the restaurant closed. The food, the wine, Miles' thoughtful company, had lifted me a little. But I knew I would have to fend for myself from then on when Miles told me he had a flight to the States early next morning.

Despite that, I headed for the room with more optimism than I'd left it with.

I hadn't told Miles what had happened on the Underground. Was it because I feared even Miles would not believe me?

Chapter 10

Sunday August 31st

Sunday August 31st

When I left the hotel early next morning, I was sure what had to be done. The night had passed slowly as I'd struggled again with the enormity of my loss. Near dawn, almost at the point of exhaustion, I'd arrived at the point I had been escaping from in the twenty years that had passed since I'd hurt that kid in the playground.

Had I been wrong to turn my back on the instincts that had been developed in me throughout childhood by the conflict in my family? Being civilised, being reasonable, depending on the law, could all have been terrible mistakes. I'd lost Julia, and there was nothing being civilised and reasonable would do to bring her back or to find those that had done this terrible thing.

And as for the law... it was in the hands of men like Hendricks.

As I entered London Bridge station, I was aware I was being followed again. The bulky man in dark clothes, now wearing a lighter jacket, was accompanied by a thinner, taller man with a scar down the length of his right cheek. They were heading straight for me. Their broad daylight intimidation was the more shocking since they appeared to be making no attempt to conceal themselves amidst the throng.

But I was not about to make the same mistake again. I took the escalator up to the main concourse at the station, heading for the most public place. I knew the station well; I was gambling they did not. In addition to the Underground, there was an overground railway with trains that ran through the station on the way to Essex and Kent and, more importantly, overground to Charing Cross.

Looking at the departures board, I could see there was a train due.

The two men continued to head for me. I wasn't sure, but I had a fear they might intend to make the hit right here and now, in front of everyone; there was something too threatening in the way they'd started to gain on me.

I knew the shops on the station concourse well. In the bookshop-cum-newsagent, there was a main entrance with automatically opening double glass doors through which most people entered and left. Fewer people knew about the second, smaller door on the other side of the store.

Timing would be everything.

The Charing Cross train had arrived at platform three and would be leaving in two minutes. That was exactly the time it would take to run from the store to the platform. Walking straight through the store, I made directly for the side door and started to run as soon as I emerged. That gave me a head start. The two assailants took a moment to realise what was happening.

As I ran across the concourse towards platform three, they were uncertain whether to give chase by running after me. There would be security cameras monitoring the coming and going of people across the concourse. There might even be full-time security people scanning the images in real time. The sight of one man running across the concourse might be taken as someone determined to catch a train. The sight of that man being chased by two others would be certain to arouse suspicion. Their actions would have been recorded and be amenable to later analysis. It was just too public and too highly observed.

I was closing in on the train on platform three. The men behind me were following but not at the same pace. They were trying to move without becoming singled out. Their aim was to move just fast enough to board the train before it departed and then to replan their attack for a more private place. I could see the train doors closing as I rounded the corner leading to the platform proper. But the rear door, where the guard stood, remained open. The guard was taking a last look up and down the platform to ensure the train was safe to depart.

It was always going to have this element of chance about it. It was always going to depend on the goodwill or indifference of the guard.

Most would just get back on the train, close the door and signal for the train to leave. This was what they'd been trained to do, on safety grounds rather than on any institutionalised sense of malice to the public. But just once in a while in a streak of humanity or of sublime indifference, the guard would let you on.

I made straight for the open door and leapt on. The guard eyed me for a moment. He must have been thinking, no doubt, he should throw me off. But maybe today it was just too much trouble; so instead, the guard just sighed and opened the connecting door that led into the passenger carriages. Indifference had won it. The guard then closed the door, rang the depart signal and waited for the train to pull out of the station. I looked back from a safe vantage point in the first carriage. I could see the two assailants rounding the corner that led onto the platform. I watched as they stood there cursing their luck as the train slowly gathered speed and edged along the platform on the way to Charing Cross.

I found a seat and thought of the plan I'd drawn up. There could be no going back. There were no easy options. I needed to work out how to get back at those who had killed Julia.

It was the only thing that mattered.

When I arrived at Charing Cross, I found an ATM, inserted my card and began drawing out money. I'd never asked the question: how much can you get from an ATM before the bank stopped the transactions? I was surprised to find I'd withdrawn £2,500 before the payments stopped. That was going to be the last time I used the credit card for the foreseeable future. Just outside the station on The Strand, I used cash to buy a pay-as-you-go phone. Untraceable, as used by criminals the world over.

I mailed to the new phone all the important messages from my existing phone, including the message from Julia that had attached the image of the Michelangelo.

I returned to the left luggage office, paid the fee and retrieved the folder containing my computer and Julia's drive. It had taken no more than a few minutes to get the cash and to do this.

Crossing The Strand, I made my way up Bow Street towards Covent Garden, pleased with the anonymity afforded by the shoppers and tourists who thronged these streets. The two assailants would have worked out I was heading for Charing Cross but by the time they arrived, I would be lost in the crowds in Covent Garden.

I moved between the shops, using only cash. I bought an anonymous zip-up travel bag and some equally anonymous casual clothes – T-shirts, jeans and sweaters, a new coat, and a pair of trainers placing them all in the bag – before heading into Covent Garden underground station in order to head to St Pancras.

As the tube exited the tunnels, I called Miles, who picked up straight away.

"Listen, Miles, I don't have much time. I'm going away. To Florence. It's something I have to do."

"I'm at the airport just about to board my flight. What's got into you?"

"Don't think it's the stress that's got me, Miles. I'll be all right; I just need time and space. Stall Hendricks if he contacts you. Tell him something. Anything that makes sense."

"It's not going to matter much what I tell him. He's not going to believe me and as sure as hell he's going to think your running away means you've got something to hide."

"Even Hendricks needs evidence. All he's got right now is a world of supposition. I don't think that will allow him to launch a manhunt."

"Jim, if I can't change your mind, then take care."

"I will." I ended the call.

As the train came into St Pancras, I left my old phone on the seat. With any luck someone would find it and use it. Then Hendricks would be tracking someone else. He might see the video footage of me running across the concourse at London Bridge station, but then the trail would go cold.

At the *Eurostar* office, after a short wait, I purchased a ticket to Paris, using cash.

On the main concourse, a monolithic, artless statue of two embracing World War II lovers stood in sharp contrast to the smaller, more human statue of John Betjeman – trench coat blowing in the wind, suitcase in hand – that graced platform 4C. The recently rebuilt overarching roof gave the whole station a feeling of grandeur, but I couldn't remain interested in such things for long. My mind was set on the short trip downstairs, the walk past the new designer store outlets and whatever awaited me as I attempted to book in for the cross-channel train to Paris.

There was an hour to kill which I spent hoping Hendricks would not have anticipated this move. I checked the passport I'd made sure to bring with me, looking at the photograph, wondering if that in itself made me look guilty. I tried to eat an anglicised version of a pasta dish at one of the concourse restaurants, but found my appetite had been drowned by the tension of waiting for the departure.

When the time came, it was simple. The border agency officer looked at the passport for only an instant. No Hendricks-inspired alarm bells sounded. In the baggage check area, I had to power-up the laptop to prove it was a working machine. They seemed more concerned with security than with who was travelling. And that was it. I was on the train and within a few minutes it would be ready to depart.

Part Two

Florence, six days earlier
Tuesday August 26th to Saturday August 30th

Chapter 11

Julia Blake left Hotel Leonardo and walked out into the incandescent heat of the narrow street that is Borgo Pinti.

Perhaps the miniskirt was a mistake. She knew she had good legs. It was hot; forty in the shade, warmer in the direct sun. It had been an impulse but one that didn't seem so bad now she could feel the way the hint of a breeze that her movement was creating in the still warm air played across the perspiration on her thighs and gave a cooling sensation.

At the end of Borgo Pinti, sitting on the shallow kerb, was a group of the homeless, drinks cans in their hands at midday. Four men, a bedraggled woman and a mangy dog. The dog began to move towards Julia and as it approached she winced; all manner of fleas and mites must be in its filthy fur. But at the last minute one of the men grabbed the dog's collar and pulled it away from her. He looked up at her. From the gutter up her skirt must have looked much too short, much too revealing. The man rolled his eyes in mock desire, knowing his days of making passes at beautiful women were long over.

The restaurant opposite, now closed, was one of the best in Florence. At night on white hot days like this they often cleared the narrow street and set tables out on the cobbles. There must have been some long established arrangement that the drunks could have that end of the street for their drinking during the day; the restaurant would have sole use of it to serve gourmet meals in the evening. No one was bothered by the contrast; the police didn't need to intervene.

It was one of the many Florentine arrangements that went on unchallenged, unofficial, unnoticed.

She crossed the busy Via dell'Oriuolo and headed for Piazza San Pier Maggiore, walking down a narrow passageway that took her past a run-down Turkish café-cum bar and out into the small square. She passed the frontage of a restaurant where outside beneath shades at neat tables tourists were surprised at their luck in finding a restaurant that served inexpensive and delicious food, while inside the locals were content the tourists were outside in the heat of the day while they were inside in the peace of the air-conditioned restaurant proper.

Turning right at the intersection with Via Ghibellina, Julia headed towards the Bargello, the ex-prison that now served as a museum, which was at the end of the street. This is where she'd agreed to meet Alessa Lando, wife of Alfieri Lando. She hardly knew what to expect. What she did know was the Landos had the most unique, varied and comprehensive collection of lesser artworks spanning the last four hundred years.

The Lando's world was secretive indeed. But if ever Julia was to find the underpaintings she was determined to convince someone like Alessa Lando she should be allowed to use her analysis techniques on a wide range of works of apparently lower rank.

She waited for her as arranged, by the statue of Caesar Augustus just inside the Bargello entrance. There was no sign of Alessa Lando. Julia had expected her to be late, as befitted someone sure of her position.

The statue of Caesar was a likeness of Cosimo de' Medici, the tyrant who had founded Renaissance Florence. The arrogance of commissioning a one-and-a-half times life size marble statue of himself as Augustus Caesar would have been difficult to understand without the knowledge of just how powerful Cosimo had been. This one statue told you more about the man and the Florentine mentality than you would ever need to know.

A voice beside her pulled her out of her reverie.

"Signora Blake," Alessa Lando said. She offered her hand and Julia shook it.

She was almost twice Julia's age, just the wrong side of sixty, dressed with the elegance expected of Italy's most wealthy. She was most likely on HRT from the look of her lineless face and neck. Her silver-grey hair spoke of money and influence.

"It's a great pleasure," Julia said.

"Shall we get coffee?" Alessa asked. "There is a place nearby."

They walked from the Bargello, crossed the street and found a quiet restaurant with tables outside shaded from the sun by a striped green awning and from the road by large shrubs in pots.

Alessa Lando must have been well-known to the restaurant owner who made a show of coming out in person to welcome her just as you would welcome the wife of a capo.

"Your proposition interests me," she began once they had ordered two espressos. "What are the chances of success?"

"That's hard to say," Julia said. "There must be a million classical paintings out there from the past four hundred years. We don't have hard evidence that any of the missing masterpieces was overpainted rather than being destroyed."

"But you must think there is a good chance, otherwise you would not be here to convince me."

"Let's say it's a matter of playing the odds. Of all the missing masterpieces, perhaps ninety-nine per cent were destroyed by fire or looting or just by general damage and dilapidation. But that leaves the one per cent and that may be overloaded with certain types of masterpieces."

"And what does that mean?" Alessa was becoming impatient.

"Controversial paintings," Julia continued, "the kind of images those in authority might want to censor as immoral or blasphemous. So, an order is made to take them away, to destroy them. But they show such undeniable beauty and the temptation must always be there to hide them and destroy something else, some lesser work, just for show, to prove it had been done. Keeping the masterpiece, trying to work out how to steal it and conceal it without it costing your life."

"And this is where your interest comes in?"

"It's one of the best ways of hiding a masterpiece – painting something on top, something innocuous. Not knowing how it would ever be revealed again but knowing that for posterity a great work had been saved."

"It would require – how do you say – courage," Alessa said.

"But there will always be people who would gamble all for beauty."

Julia could feel Alessa Lando taking her in, scrutinising her body, glancing down at the expanse of skin, her long legs only partially concealed beneath the table. And in that moment she felt not only disapproval but also a strong premonition of danger.

"I think something brought you to me," Alessa said. She reached forward and held her hand. "Sometimes our lives are influenced by the fate that works without our knowledge."

In another woman's mouth this might have seemed like female bonding. There was something in Alessa Lando's manner that turned this into menace.

"The paintings, Signora Lando."

"Alessa, please."

"Alessa."

"Yes, the paintings. If you found a Michelangelo or a da Vinci…"

"It would be priceless," Julia said. She thought that the promise of hundreds of millions was, more than anything, the spur needed for the Landos to forsake their obsessive demand for privacy.

"So you want to scan the Lando collection?"

Alessa Lando was hooked.

"Yes. It won't harm your pictures, but it will allow me see the outline of any painting that lies beneath."

"And to find a masterpiece?"

"Yes, even from the faintest outline. I have a computer program. I have fed it scans of just about all of the known missing masterpieces and existing works by the same artists for comparison. It will make the comparison for us. If there is any similarity with the underpainting, it will pick it up straight away."

"And the method is completely without… damage?"

"Terahertz imaging. It's completely non-destructive. It's essentially the same technique they are beginning to use at airports to look for hidden items."

"And what is the deal?"

"50-50 if I find a hidden masterpiece."

"70-30," Alessa said. "After all, my family owns the paintings."

"OK, 70-30. I have a contract drawn up. We can both sign."

"And you'll be able to remove the other painting?"

"It will be difficult," Julia said. "But with time and care it can be done."

"Very well, Signora Blake. We have a deal." She held out her hand again in an elaborate show of formality.

Julia shook her hand. "We have a deal." She pulled papers from her bag, quickly wrote in the agreed revenue split, and offered them to her. "Two copies of the agreement", she smiled. "Read it over and sign if you approve."

"I am sure we can trust each other," Alessa said, as she placed the papers in her bag.

With a timing that could not be coincidence, a black BMW with tinted windows drew up outside the restaurant. Julia was then aware everything they'd been doing was being watched. Alessa must have made the slightest signal and the car had arrived. An overweight man in a baggy dark suit got out while his companion, a thin, craggy-faced man with a long scar running down the left hand side of his face, stayed behind the wheel.

"Thank you, Giuseppe," Alessa said. The burly man held open the car door for her.

Julia tried to smile, as the fat man looked her up and down. She couldn't see his eyes beneath his wraparound sunglasses but she had the feeling that if she could have seen them she would not have liked the look to be found there.

"I'll be in touch," Alessa said. She settled into the back seat of the car and it drove off.

They hadn't discussed how they would meet again nor where she was staying but Julia was left in no doubt they already knew enough about her to contact her any time they liked.

Chapter 12

Emelia Rossellini walked across Piazza San Pier Maggiore, past the restaurant with the tourists at the outside tables.

She just couldn't work out how it had to come to this.

She loved Matteo and she was sure he must really love her the way it had been when they'd started going together. He'd been kind and had shown her every consideration. He'd bought her clothes and jewellery and paid for the best beauty salons available anywhere in Florence. When she first met him she was nothing. Nothing but the beauty Matteo saw in her. They'd made exquisite love, just not being able to get enough of each other. And the cocaine they'd begun snorting together just heightened it all and made each orgasm seem never ending.

And then it had started to change. Slowly at first, he'd started to draw away from her, testing her love, breaking her heart, making her more dependent on him. Keeping back the cocaine until she did as he asked. Until it was not even a shock when he'd asked her to sleep with one of his friends. Looking back, this had been the moment when he'd turned her into his whore. Not in a low life way, but with finesse and charm and due account to the finer things in life. A high-class whore for a high-class clientele.

Why couldn't she just walk away? She still loved Matteo even though he'd become her pimp. For just a single shadow of the love they'd shared in the early days, she would do almost anything he wanted.

And then there was the cocaine. Could you get addicted to cocaine? After all this time she would have to admit she didn't really know. It didn't seem like a physical addiction like that to cigarettes or heroin, so she'd heard. You felt you might be able to do without it. And yet the high was so good it kept drawing you back to it, making you crave for a moment of intensity that, though it grew shorter each time you came to it, nevertheless was irresistible.

She was going to meet Zella, the woman who had a hand in so much that Alfieri Lando did. She fixed her up with her clients. She kept the cocaine, rationed it, kept it back until she'd done the day's business. She couldn't afford to fall foul of Zella, this was the simple fact of her existence.

Zella DeFrancesco was waiting, as arranged, sitting in the back of a black BMW with tinted windows.

"You're late," Zella said. Emelia got in. "But you look good. You've been taking my advice and looking after yourself."

"I know," Emelia said. "A special client." She'd heard nothing but talk of preparation for this special client. For over ten days she hadn't been asked to sleep with anyone. She'd been told to rest and eat and beautify herself. To get ready for this most important man.

"So today it's here." Zella smiled. "We go there straight away."

Chapter 13

Walking back to the Bargello, Julia went straight upstairs to the large exhibition space. There, lying on its face, suspended on an open trellis structure lay Donatello's *David*. It was surrounded by all manner of conservation tools and at the head of the area there were display boards that sought to explain what was happening to this, the world's most valuable life-size sculpture. Compared with the better-known statue of *David* by Michelangelo it was diminutive, feminine.

Dressed in a white coat and concentrating hard on a minute area the centre of the *David's* back, Anna Pini didn't see Julia arriving.

She was employing many of the latest analysis and restoration tools on this most valuable object. Lasers were being used to scan the sculpture to record in minute detail its shape and topography, generating a 3-D image that could be rotated, magnified and presented as surface relief data to expand knowledge of the work. Lasers were also being used to vaporise small regions of the surface to provide chemical analysis via spectroscopy. And lasers were being used with great care and alongside other more conventional methods to restore regions on the black metallic surface that were corroded. It was an impressive display of what these new techniques could achieve.

Perhaps this was compensation for the disappointment of the visitors who came to the Bargello specifically to see the Donatello only to find it removed from display.

"Anna!" Julia shouted. "Don't you ever stop working?"

Anna stopped, looked up and smiled. She'd known Julia for over three years now, since their meeting at a conference on laser conservation in Rome. She'd heard that Julia had returned to Florence and had been looking forward to making contact with her again.

Anna said, "The Donatello is intractable. I'll be working on it to almost the end of the year!"

"Rewarding, though?"

"Yes, but requiring so much patience. I can feel the resentment rising. Why spend so much time on this? Why can't we see the *David* now? That's why they put me out there in the middle of the gallery, so all those frustrated visitors can see work is being done."

"And that's what you find stressful?"

"Of course. Trying to carry out complex conservation before an audience is never easy. An audience that only wants you to get on with it and get out of the way."

They laughed together.

"I thought you must have been avoiding me," she said.

"Of course not." Julia gave her friend a welcoming hug. "I've been busy, tracking down a source of paintings, and I think I just might have succeeded."

Anna knew of Julia's abiding interest. There was almost no one in the field who didn't know just how committed Julia was to finding her masterpiece. "A gallery?"

"No, an individual. You may know of her – Alessa Lando has given me access to the Lando's entire collection."

Instead of the expected delight that her friend had finally found a source of paintings for her search, Anna looked surprised and shocked. "Lando." She was trying to suppress a note of distaste in her voice. "What on earth made you go to them?"

"They have the paintings, all of the right type, all those later lesser works that are prime candidates for having been overpainted."

"You might see it differently if you lived in Florence as long as I have. You see too much of Florence through the eyes of an innocent and that could be very dangerous. A man like Alfieri Lando has a reputation that is deserved. If only half of what is rumoured is true, you are placing yourselves in the hands of a very dangerous family indeed."

Julia thought of the car – its tinted windows, the way it suddenly appeared outside the pavement restaurant, the burly minder and his scarred accomplice, her own feelings of danger.

She knew Anna was not exaggerating but she didn't want to be dissuaded after spending so long tracking down such a good source of material for her search.

"I was sure Alessa was not going to buy into it but I think the thought of all the money she might make was in the end too much for her."

"Yes, I'm surprised, Julia. You must have been persuasive. Absolute secrecy is their normal way."

"I don't think she intends to involve her husband much," Julia said. "He doesn't have any interest in art. The paintings are hers, essentially. He's indifferent to them and anything I might do."

"Is that what she told you?"

"I think he would only get interested once we'd found something worth a great deal of money."

Anna was about to disagree but would only say, "Keep away from him, that's my strong advice."

"You'd better tell me what you mean."

It was time for Anna's break, so they found a quiet table in the corner of the staff coffee area and Julia listened carefully as Anna told her what she knew about Alessa and Alfieri Lando and their family.

The power in the family had been with Alfieri and his ancestors as long as anyone could recall. Theirs was one of the oldest families in Florence with a history stretching back over five hundred years. But Alessa had established her influence as a matriarch in controlling the public image of the Landos and in particular in seeking to limit the excesses of her husband. He'd sought to break her influence. They now lived largely apart; she at their property in Lucca and he on their estate on the outskirts of Florence and in an apartment in town. They were united now only in competition for the affections of their only child Matteo and for maximising the proceeds of the family businesses, most of which would have failed the test of legitimacy if given any form of scrutiny.

Alessa Lando's background was Argentinian and obscured by rumour. Certainly the Lando family already had wealth before she'd married Alfieri. But she'd brought with her a considerable fortune. While the source of the existing Lando wealth did not require much speculation, there was mystery over the origins of Alessa's. However you looked at it, the Landos were dangerous and Julia needed to face up quickly to the type of people she was dealing with. That explained the urgency of Anna's comments.

"Just promise me you won't get drawn into something you will come to regret," she said.

"Of course," Julia said. "I'll be careful."

Chapter 14

Emelia always asked for a snort of coke at this moment and it was always refused. But today, Zella reached into a pocket and brought out the little white sachet that meant so much.

"Yes, use all you need, we want you to be at your very best." Taking out the mirror from her cosmetics bag, Emelia laid out a line of white powder. Using a cigarette holder she kept in the bag and carefully dividing the line into two, she snorted one half into each nostril, feeling the euphoria crazing through her bloodstream.

"There will be another bag when you get there," Zella DeFrancesco said.

The car drew up outside an apartment facing the deep-sided river Arno. The building wasn't much to look at on the outside but once they came out of the lift at the third floor Emelia was taken by the sudden transformation to opulence. They rang at a heavy door and it was opened by a young man dressed in black, too well-dressed and too physically strong to be a mere house servant. He led them into a marble furnished room and beyond that into a bedroom the centrepiece of which was an erotically styled red couch. Emelia knew straight away what the couch was for; the way the curves of the couch were angled, no sexual position was unreachable.

"Ah, the love couch," Zella said. "All the way from America; a special treat for our special client."

Emelia approached the couch with caution.

"Don't be afraid of it, Emelia. You will enjoy it, I know."

"I don't think I'm ready for this," Emelia said. "I want to call it off."

"No need to be so afraid. You want to please us all, don't you? This is important to him. And this may help." Zella reached in her pocket and pulled out another small white bag.

Emelia stopped. If it wasn't an addiction, why was she so irresistibly drawn to the small white packet? She took the bag and snorted two more lines from her mirror. The hit was stronger than before, coming on top of the lines she'd snorted in the car. She could feel herself becoming woozy, sinking into that white oblivion.

Only half-aware, she was lifted onto the red couch and her clothes were removed, to be replaced by a red robe. The man in the dark suit had gone but Zella remained. A door opened and a man wearing a long cape and a mask came in. He looked at her for some long moment, taking in the beauty of her body. Zella was standing there, stroking Emelia's hand, telling her to relax and enjoy. She wanted to resist; everything was unnatural about what was happening, but the coke had really kicked in and she could feel only the onrushing euphoria of the double hit and Zella's soothing voice saying everything was fine.

Within a minute he was inside her, standing over her as she lay back on the couch. She could feel the cape that he wore enveloping her. She could hear his breaths turning into grunts and sighs as he became engorged by his lust.

Even deep within the coke trance, there was something familiar about that voice. Where had she heard it? Was it really Matteo coming back to her at last? And then in a moment of exertion, as he turned her over on the couch to enter her from behind, the mask slipped and, before he could replace it, Emelia saw the face of Alfieri Lando, Matteo's father, contorted and lecherous.

She lay there, pretending not to have seen him, faking orgasm as she'd learned to do even from within the coke haze.

Her mind was shutting down. Only one thought remained. Did Matteo know?

Chapter 15

Julia had been right; they knew exactly where to find her. The very next morning, following the meeting with Alessa Lando, the fat man who had been introduced as Giuseppe was waiting for her in the lobby of Hotel Leonardo.

"Buongiorno, Signora Blake," he said with an expression that was more a leer than a smile. "Signora Lando asked me to take care of you."

Julia tried to concentrate on what had to be done. "I made arrangements with my sponsors at the university to have a loan of their scanning equipment; I have it for a week only, I hope that will be enough time."

Giuseppe drove. They called at the university, picked up the portable terahertz scanning system, loaded it into the back of the car and set out for the Lando estate, an hour's drive away on the outskirts of Lucca. Julia sat uncomfortably in the back seat of the car, trying to avoid her gaze falling on the glistening folds of skin on the back of the neck of the overweight man as he concentrated on steering the car. There was little conversation; just the sound of the inane Italian pop music he was playing on the radio.

As they pulled onto the Viareggio-bound A11 Autostrada that streamed the traffic out of Florence, the outer suburbs gave way quickly to classic views of the Tuscan countryside – gently sloping hillsides planted with vines, olives and Cyprus trees; the occasional glimpse of a red-roofed village tucked away on higher ground; shades of green and yellow intensified by the bright summer sunshine. Life might be simpler here, Julia thought, but almost certainly much harder in the stifling heat outside of the air-conditioned environment of the car.

She thought about her own comfortable upbringing as the daughter of an Irish dentist, then settled in Guilford. Always given the best and simply expected to succeed from the very start of her life, there could not have been any doubt success would follow. Excellence at sports and straight A's in everything she had studied had led, as expected, to a place at Cambridge where she hadn't been outshone by the very best the English schooling system – state or private – could throw up. The double First in Art History and Classics had surprised no one. And her Masters in Art Conservation was a natural follow on that led to her PhD and the post at the Restoration Studio. But somehow she was still hung up on success. Was that what she was still chasing, still seeking to make her name by discovering something so important that everyone would have to recognise she was at the top of the tree?

She had to admit that her success so far hadn't been enough. There was an emptiness there waiting to be filled, something sensed but incapable of intellectualisation despite her degrees and her determination to root it out. It was an unease that came most nights as she waked from incomplete sleep. Something nagging her, something she could feel but could not touch.

Of course, there was Jim, something that was just meant to be. A love that was quiet and unboastful and eloquent and everything she wanted it to be. There would be children one day. That would be wonderful. But without undermining her love for Jim and his love for her, she knew none of this would take away the nagging feeling of emptiness. Perhaps after all this was what was driving her on in her search, some way of breaking through from subterranean feeling to the bright light of day.

They'd already reached Coppanori, just fifteen minutes outside of Lucca. Giuseppe was pulling off the Autostrada, heading off down narrower country roads. It was time to gather her thoughts for the day ahead.

The Lando house was a large Palladian-style residence set in several acres of wooded grounds, protected by high walls, security cameras and, no doubt, although Julia couldn't immediately see them, security staff to repel unwanted visitors.

When they arrived Giuseppe produced the agreement duly signed in two copies by Alessa Lando. Julia looked over both, giving one back to him and putting the other in her bag. "Everything in place," she said, but Giuseppe remained as uncommunicative as ever as he tucked the Lando copy of the agreement into his inside breast pocket.

Once they had the scanning equipment set up in the small anteroom on the ground floor, it was a question of care in removing each painting from its hanging position, placing it on the bed of the machine, selecting the correct exposure and scanning parameters from the computer and standing by as the scan head moved slowly over the surface.

Not much different to making a photocopy. Just slower, and with a beam that could 'see' beneath the surface of the painting. Giuseppe, as he'd no doubt been instructed to do, followed her every move.

"Alessa is not around?" Julia asked as he watched her set up the next painting for scanning.

"She will be spending the day in Venice," Giuseppe said without any further explanation.

"And Signor Lando?"

"He's never here now. Spends most of his time at the other house near Firenze."

Julia was disappointed at not meeting Alfieri Lando. She would have liked to make up her own mind about the Lando patriarch and not just be dependent on the rumours relayed to her by Anna.

The Landos had a collection more extensive than Julia had supposed. There were areas in the twenty-room house given over completely to paintings, filling every inch of wall space. There were some two hundred paintings in all and by the end of the first day she'd completed just over eighty.

"Same time tomorrow," Julia said as Giuseppe dropped her back at the hotel at the end of the day. He nodded, smiled insincerely, and drove away.

Julia sat for some moments in the hotel lobby, trying to shift the feeling of unease from her mind. Why was it that the perfectly routine matter of scanning the Lando's paintings should be so unnerving?

She thought about Jim again, what he must have been doing that day back in London, how much she loved him and missed him and how her determination to make a name for herself in the art world was leading them to be spending so much time apart. Somehow that was part of the unease. Though she couldn't quite define it, she felt she was entering into a course of events that would place even greater distance between them.

Trying to call him was unsuccessful. Why wouldn't he keep his phone switched on? OK, he was in a production studio at the radio station for most of the day and you had to have your phone switched off, but he was notoriously bad at answering missed calls. She would have to e-mail him.

She hooked into her computer using the hotel Wi-Fi hotspot, emailing Jim and, as a matter of habit, encrypting and saving to her hard drive.

> Jim. Missing you. Everything going well here. I think I'm getting close to the endpoint. Will be home soon, love, Julia.

She knew that was right. If only she could have spoken to him, she could have edged up to the idea of the ever present but not so easy to define sense of apprehension she could not dislodge. But there was no way she could put that into an e-mail. It was true what they said. Don't send anything contentious by e-mail; it will make the subtle seem crass and the inferred seem bold. No use worrying him. It would all work out.

But behind the steady logic she knew must be right, she felt desperately alone and in need of his touch.

Chapter 16

She lay on the bed in the small apartment, crying, aching, hurting.

It was physical and it was mental. The rape had been brutal and since she'd been drugged and shorn of any normal response, the physical hurt had been great indeed. It felt like her insides had been gouged out. He'd been big, too big, of a size that never really could have been capable of any normal love.

Emelia tried to get up from the bed but could hardly walk.

But this was only physical. The hurt in her mind was greater. Why had Matteo allowed her to be used in this way? What kind of punishment was it to have her raped by his own father? What had she done to earn such treatment? She only loved Matteo. All she'd done, everywhere her life had led, had been to please him, to be with him, to love him.

And Zella? She must have known. She had led her there to the apartment. She'd made the arrangement; she'd been there: she too must share the shame.

What did they think? Did they think she wouldn't know who it was?

They must think she was stupid and too gone on coke to care. And that made things worse; the thought they considered themselves so powerful they could do this to her and there would be no comeback. This in the end was the real hurt; that they could abuse her in this way without any thought, because she was nothing; that they expected she would go on taking whatever humiliation they wanted to throw at her. Because they were sure she was so totally in their power, so dependent on them, they could do anything they wanted with her.

It hadn't always been like this. She'd been young. She'd been talented. More than one person had told her that as she'd fought her way out of small town Brindisi and into the rat-race of the fashion world in Milan. She could have been a designer; that had been her goal. But then one day a photographer had stopped her as she walked down the street and told her she should have a career in modelling. And she'd developed a portfolio and auditioned for the agencies that served the fashion houses and for a while it had been genuinely glamorous. It had led her to Matteo who had seen her, wooed her, brought her to Florence and led her, by degrees, to the place where she now was.

When she looked back, she knew she would remember this moment as the point where she fell out of love with Matteo. The point where love turned to hatred of the most determined kind. She saw in that moment what you fail to see when submerged in the warm comfort of love itself; the devious, self-serving, duplicitous actions of a man bent only on making her little more than his slave. What anyone but she could plainly see. What she now saw with blinding clarity.

She was weak; she knew that. But from this point of weakness, from this point of utter desolation beneath which she could not further sink, Emelia Rossellini vowed revenge, on Alfieri Lando, his son Matteo Lando and their servant Zella DeFrancesco.

The Landos had all the power. But she'd seen beneath the mask and knew it had been Alfieri Lando who had hurt her in this way. That knowledge, and the fact this was a secret they were unaware she knew, was the key she would use to bring them all down.

What hurt, beyond all else, was that Matteo didn't care. When she'd called him he'd been cold. He wouldn't even see her. Said he was busy! Busy all week working for his father.

She had almost no one to turn to; only one person. Of all the men Matteo had made her go with there was only one who seemed to care.

She picked up the phone and dialled.

"Giancarlo. Thank God you're there."

Chapter 17

In the large town house on the outskirts of Florence, Alfieri Lando was finishing his third espresso of the morning.

"Matteo, what is your dear mother up to right now?" he said. He was demanding an answer from his son who was sitting opposite him at a long oak table.

"Nothing to worry about," Matteo said. "Just the usual, trying to check up on what we have both been doing. Trying to make sure we don't betray the honour of the family."

"She's taking care of the legitimate businesses as normal?"

"Yes, that, and she's burying herself in the world of art; in all those paintings she has out at Lucca."

Alfieri showed his teeth in the disguise of a smile. "If it keeps her out of my hair, it's worth encouraging her interest."

"Zella tells me she has a specialist from England looking at the paintings."

"So long as we can get on with our business."

His father spent the next hour detailing how he wanted the operation to be run that day, just as he did every day. He itemised every unfortunate businessman or trader who had to be squeezed, every dealer who had to deliver, every construction deal that had to go down. But Matteo's thoughts were elsewhere.

Matteo hadn't liked the recent happenings with Emelia. In that Alfieri had given him no choice. So he shouldn't care about it for too long.

It had always been like this; he'd been raised by a father who demanded everything from him while pretending he was giving everything to him. Outside the family, everyone thought he'd been over-indulged and that was why he would always be in the shadow of his father. But the truth was far worse. No one knew the level of terror in which he'd been raised nor the intensity of his father's anger, the constant threat to conform to his father's wishes, even in the smallest things. What colours he should like. How he should eat. What style to cut his hair. The length of his fingernails. When and when not to smile. Never to cry. Never to show fear. Never to show weakness. How to look strong. What he should think.

No one knew of the furious rages his father was capable of over even the smallest indiscretion. Getting the smallest thing wrong had brought a world of wrath and pain descending upon him. It had ruined the idea of trust and had made the possibility of love a remote thing. It made him almost incapable of showing any true emotion, as emotions too had been the subject of censure; don't give any chance to others to find a point weakness, this had been the constant place at which he'd been tested over and over.

Worst of all, the feeling now that after twenty-three years of torture at the hands of his father he was becoming just like him; heartless, ruthless, godlike. It was happening and he didn't like it. At least this perhaps was a source of hope; that he knew this, and Alfieri had not quite succeeded in making him in his own image.

Yet his father had made him kill for him. The first time, when he was eighteen, it had been as much as anything a test of loyalty. The businessman who had got in Alfieri's way and had been asked to step aside and allow his business to be taken over for a building development and who instead had publicly insulted Alfieri. It had fallen to Matteo to prove his loyalty that first time by killing the man. And now he had killed, what was it, eight times, not now in the name of loyalty but because this was what he was expected to do.

So finding Emelia, wooing her, loving her, breaking her heart, turning her out onto the street and giving her to his father was no more painful than anything else he'd been required to do.

Yet it was still difficult, after all he'd been through, to understand the heartlessness of his father when it came to Emelia. Yes, it was true that Emelia's father, Empirio Rossellini, had been a rival in the battle to control the drugs trade in Milan and Florence. Their battle had been a matter of life and death. But Alfieri had won; surely this should have been satisfaction enough; to have Empirio and his key sidemen gunned down, to have the remnants of his family displaced in shame to the South of Italy, surely that should have been enough for any man, despite the damage caused to both sides when the battle had raged.

But, twenty years later, to task Matteo with hunting down Empirio's daughter, bringing her to Florence and turning her out as a whore was the hard edge of revenge indeed. Emelia hadn't been difficult to find; neighbours in Brindisi had been all too ready to tell Matteo about the beautiful young woman who had gone to Milan to pursue a career in fashion design. Though the family had kept the same name, Emelia, like her brothers, had been raised without knowing anything about their father's past and the battle with the Landos; an attempt to make a fresh start, unsullied by those treacherous events.

In Milan, it hadn't been difficult to call in a favour with a photographer to discover her as if by chance one day on the street and to task him with launching her modelling career. And it hadn't been difficult for Matteo to then meet her, again as if by chance, and convince her he loved her and to bring her to Florence.

For Alfieri, his father, to want to rape Emelia, as he'd done in the apartment overlooking the Arno, was the kind of cruel celebration of victory in the battle with the Rossellinis that Matteo had come to loathe but to expect. Videoing the rape was a step too far. He felt sickened, despite all his father had done to subvert his emotions over the twenty-three years of his life.

He knew he couldn't seek help from his mother, Alessa. She would blame him for having gone along with Alfieri's wishes. No, as always when he felt troubled, he would have to talk this over with Zella.

"You know what we need to do," Alfieri said. "Make sure it is done."

Chapter 18

Sitting in the small restaurant of the Peggy Guggenheim Gallery on the Grand Canal in Venice, Zella DeFrancesco was deep in thought. It was one of the places she could not help but keep returning to. She liked to imagine the scandal Peggy had caused living here with Max Ernst and Alberto Giacometti. She would have liked to have lived like that, to be as wild and as free as Peggy, but she had Alfieri and the burden of the Lando family to cope with and she couldn't think of a time when she would be free from that. But she loved to come here and marvel at the thick sensuous paint on the Max Ernst paintings displayed so intimately on the walls of the gallery. Until she'd seen them she had no idea of the depth of the imagination at work, no idea of the challenge to reason posed by *Attirement of the Bride* nor how these images served as a metaphor for her own life.

Still, it amused her to watch the tourists as they walked out onto the terrace overlooking the Grand Canal and first noticed Marino Marini's statue *The Angel of the City* looking out over the water. From behind it looked innocent enough; an almost life-size depiction of a man astride a horse, his arms held out shoulder high at his sides, his head raised aloft.

Zella never tired of being intrigued by the expressions of the tourists as they realised that the man, when viewed from any other angle, could be seen to have a thoroughly prominent erection.

Marini had lived and worked in Florence. Where else? This was Florence's take on the world distilled with such precision into a single gesture. The rider erect as he stared out over the Grand Canal, daring anyone to take away his right to take on the world any way he chose. If she'd been a filmmaker she would have made a documentary with a hidden camera showing the expression on the faces of the nurses and lawyers and shop workers and pensioners as they realised what their eyes were seeing. But she was no filmmaker. She was here for business and Alessa Lando was late.

There would be difficult times ahead, Zella knew that. A centre of balance was shifting and she was becoming more concerned than she'd been in years. Alfieri had been lucky in his life almost without having to try. He'd found Alessa. She had money in her family; no one was sure where it came from but it had been there in abundance. And he'd used the money to enhance his power, the power to have almost anything he wanted. Alessa had been beautiful but time had taken take care of that. And he had Matteo, the child who had been promised everything but who most now thought would amount to nothing but a pale shadow of his father. Yes, there was some fairness, some balance in this.

And then there was Emelia. So unfair that she was so beautiful. No women should have the potential of that sort of power over men just by looking the way they do. Zella had seen to that; maintained the supply of coke, helped

Matteo to let her go, broken her hold over him, created a situation where he was happy to do as his father wished and turn her out as a high-class whore. Her beauty would fade more rapidly than any natural ageing process. Yes, there was fairness and balance in this too.

Matteo himself; how unlucky to have been raised by Alfieri and Alessa. Given everything, raised in such expectation, given every advantage, expected to have the world at his feet, anything and everything he wanted. Fate had settled that score by itself. He was set on the path where he would amount to nothing.

Alessa arrived, late as always. She sat opposite Zella at the table and when the waiter arrived she ordered her customary macchiato. "I was held up at the furriers. Such wonderful sable, I just had to go inside and look."

"You bought something?" Zella asked.

"Ordered it. I have to wait for the next shoot and the hanging of the pelts before they can make the coat. So I had a preliminary fitting."

Zella could not help thinking the prospect of all those deaths was the real attraction of the coat for Alessa. "So a month?"

"Two or three. It's getting harder to find the little darlings. Too many of those environmentalists and their simple-minded protection of endangered species. It slows the whole thing down. But next winter I'll be the one who's happiest – content *and* warm."

It was good that Alessa was so sure Zella was her confidante. The idea of going to Venice, where the prying eyes of Alfieri's men would not follow them, strengthened this illusion.

Alessa's change of tone suggested it was time to get down to business. "So, what news do you have for me?"

"Matteo needs help." Zella gave a well-rehearsed look of concern. "There's a young girl, I suppose you'd call her beautiful. He has, well, an attachment stronger than he would like to admit. If she wasn't a Rossellini."

"A Rossellini," Alessa spat. "Matteo must know he can't have anything to do with anyone from that family."

"Emelia Rossellini. She's attractive."

"I forbid it. I'm sure Alfieri thinks the same on this."

Zella had raised a concern that seemed to have hit home. Alessa Lando spent most of the remaining time asking Zella everything she knew about Emelia. She deliberately left out the fact that Emelia was working as a whore in the expectation that when Alessa discovered this for herself, as she would fairly easily, she would be more enraged than if this had come out at the start.

"You did right to let me know," Alessa said, once she was sure she'd extracted all she needed.

"There's something else," Zella said. "The English woman you have looking at the family paintings…"

"Julia Blake?"

"I have it on good authority she might not be all she seems, not just a conservator."

"Then what?"

"Someone seeking to investigate the Lando family from the inside. Maybe an agent for an enemy of the family."

"Not police? Not tax evasion?"

"I don't know. Could be something more sinister. That's all I've heard."

"Where did you get this?"

"It was from Albertini in the Justice Ministry. They've started some investigations but he wouldn't say any more."

Zella was pleased Dino Albertini had agreed to investigate Julia Blake when she'd phoned him. It was a favour in return for Alfieri helping to fix his promotion that she had been waiting to call in.

There was no doubting Alessa's concern. But she said little more, suddenly preferring at this point to keep her thoughts to herself. Zella felt she'd touched a nerve, though she was secretly pleased the tactic had achieved such a strong effect.

Yes, Zella thought, the balance was shifting.

What no one knew was that the Landos and the Rossellinis had ruined her life. It had taken years to overcome the grief at what they'd done to her and, difficult though it had been, another five years to work her way into a position of confidence with Alfieri and Alessa.

It would have not been too difficult, given that she was now on the inside, to find a way of killing them both. But that would only lead to their replacement by others just as ruthless. No, she was determined to avenge the deaths of those that were so dear to her by engineering the downfall of the whole family. She would settle for nothing less. And in Matteo she saw the agent of that destruction.

Emelia was part of the Rossellini family. Zella blamed them just as much as the Landos and had found it easy to collude in Emelia's downfall. And now that the rape had taken place, Zella was sure it would not be long before Matteo was asking for her advice once again.

Chapter 19

Giancarlo met Emelia on the corner of Via Ricasoli and Via degli Alfani, quiet streets just a short walk away from the Academia. He hadn't told her why he'd suggested they meet there.

She'd been crying, he could see that. "You all right?"

"Not really," she said. "Why are we meeting here?"

"There is something I want to show you." He took her arm and walked her along Via Ricasoli towards the Academia.

They didn't make it easy for locals like Emelia to see inside. Most days the museum was besieged by tourists waiting for up to an hour to get in. But Giancarlo had a pass and that meant they could just walk in past the lines. Emelia didn't complain but it was clear she was apprehensive about where he was taking her.

"Why here? Why here?" was all she would say.

Giancarlo moved them on through the entrance hall and, in a few short minutes, they were standing in the Gallery of Slaves, the long corridor-like space that housed Michelangelo Buonarotti's unfinished sculptures – partially completed figures trapped in the huge blocks of stone from which it seemed they'd failed to escape. They had been donated by Michelangelo to Cosimo de' Medici after they'd been turned down by the Vatican for Pope Julius II's mausoleum.

Emelia stood and stared. Giancarlo didn't say a word. She knew immediately why he'd brought her here. Yes, he thought her life was little more than that of a modern day slave, no different from the life of those souls trapped in those blocks of stone. She caressed the form of the Awakening Slave, running her hands over the cold, hard stone, feeling how the body shape had been worked out of the hidden structure of the stone, feeling the tool marks left behind as Michelangelo's chisels struck with such precision all those years ago. And she began to cry.

Giancarlo was concerned the gallery staff would have them removed for touching the sculptures but in the event, no one came.

"So you brought me here, to show me this, to tell me my life is no better than this?" The anger in her voice matched the tears in her eyes. "Is this some new way you have found to drive me further down?"

"It's not designed to make you feel worse about yourself."

"Then why bring me here to tell me something I should already know? Don't you think this is humiliating? Nothing to lose, eh?"

"That's not what I'm trying to say." He tried to hold her but she pulled away.

"And I am so much the slave that I wouldn't understand any of this if you hadn't brought me here?"

"Look up," Giancarlo said. He'd managed to place his arm around her and was pointing her towards the statue of David in the circular gallery beyond. "What do you see?"

Michelangelo's statue of David, fully three times life-size, rising high above the surrounding tourists, looked back.

"We trap ourselves. We make slaves of ourselves," he whispered. "We make our own chains. The powerful look on without a care, inflated by the pride made possible by our entrapment."

"And the *David* looks down on the gallery of slaves, and it's been like this for as long as anyone can remember," she said. "Where is the hope in that?"

She looked at him and he could see the anguish in her eyes. "And you are no different. You use me and abuse me just like them. Why should I care if the sight of art gives you an excuse to seek to ease your conscience?"

"It doesn't have to be like that," Giancarlo said. "I'd never have known you if we hadn't both been as we are, here and now."

"You mean, if I was not a whore you pay and choose not to screw."

"If you had not been driven to this by the Landos and all they stand for."

"So why do you care?" she asked. "What makes you want to stand up for we poor slaves?"

"You want what I want," he said. "We have a common cause. To bring the Landos down. To put an end to that arrogance."

She didn't know if she could trust him. It came as a surprise; after all he'd been the only person she could turn to, yet there was still the fear, ever present, that this might be a trap. It was hurting her to think this but she couldn't tell if this was not some cleverly conceived plot by Matteo to test her loyalty.

"Why should I be interested in any of this? You know I'm Matteo's, that I belong to him."

Giancarlo looked back at her; his eyes were saying he didn't believe what she was saying.

"You don't know whether you can trust me."

"We know each other, Gianni. But I don't have any idea who you really are, any more than you really know who I am."

"So there can be no trust amongst the slaves?"

"Maybe that's what explains why things have been as they are for so long." She attempted a smile. "So, what do you want, Gianni? Always assuming I might help you."

"Information. Something I can use to bring the Landos down."

Emelia nodded. She knew what he was suggesting was anything but easy. She had to take a chance, she knew it, if she was to begin to repay Alfieri for the harm he'd done. The thought of that made the risk worth taking even though she knew the price of failure was in reality too high.

Giancarlo said no more. It was time to leave; the gallery would soon be closing.

Chapter 20

There was always a risk in trying to play Alfieri Lando; Zella knew that. He was intrinsically suspicious of everyone and everything, a paranoia that passed for normality in those that kept their power only by making many enemies. It was born of the realisation that for all the men and women who had been beaten or killed over the last thirty years, there were brothers and sisters, children and distant family members who would have thoughts of revenge. In the face of immediate and extreme violence, most people back down, but there was always the possibility someone would mistakenly risk all and take a chance. No, given the numbers involved it was more or less certain someone would. So the paranoia was all the worse for having a rational foundation.

Alfieri had called Zella into his study where she found Matteo also waiting. They must be going over the results of the day's business as they always did at this time of evening. Alfieri looked up as she came in. He clearly had things on his mind.

"You remember Albertini?" He spoke slowly, drawing out the words.

She tried to look as if she could hardly recall him. "You mean the guy in the Interior Ministry?"

"Yes that's him. We helped him with his last promotion, you recall. A job for Matteo in the end. A superior who would not retire early as he should have done and who ended up having to retire on health grounds after all."

Matteo was trying to erase the memory of the beating he'd given the elderly civil servant; the crunch of the knuckledusters on the old man's nose as it had shattered.

"Albertini's path to promotion was suddenly unblocked." Alfieri smiled. "He was, and of course remains, grateful for our help."

"Of course," Zella said.

"So it was a surprise when he told me you had asked him for a favour."

"Oh, that," she said. She was trying to make it seem matter-of-fact.

"No one calls in favours but me!" He was agitated by Zella's attempt to shrug this off. "Did you really think no one would find out?"

"I had a special reason," Zella said. Why hadn't she worked out that Albertini would contact Alfieri making sure he'd been released from his obligation? That was so foreseeable. That could be the difference between life and death. "There is a problem with Alessa and I had to think of something to divert her sudden interest in Emelia."

She could see Alfieri taking this in, weighing the truthfulness or otherwise of what she'd just said.

"She knows about what took place in the apartment?"

"No, of course not, but she is getting closer. She has that Giuseppe monster of hers sniffing around. She is beginning to ask questions about Emelia, suspecting she is in a relationship with Matteo, thinking first it is inappropriate and then it is a sham, a cover for something more. She is getting close to guessing the truth and I had to invent a diversion. I told her the English woman, the one testing her paintings, was a spy. I had to arrange for some sort of corroboration or she would not have believed me. So I thought of Albertini and how he owed us a favour and I asked him to check if Julia Blake was a problem."

Alfieri had clearly been set back by the thought that Alessa may have been getting close to finding out about his predilections.

"You should have come to me first. I would have given you permission to use Albertini."

"There wasn't time. I had to find a story that would hold her attention. It seems to have worked. She's spooked. She has men running around following the Blake woman and everything she does. She's going to be closing down the scanning operation on the paintings."

"I never liked the idea of her messing with the family paintings," Alfieri said. "Alessa has begun using some of our men in London; she asked permission for that, just as you should have done."

"I'm sorry."

"Don't try anything like that again."

"And Albertini?"

"I told him he still owed us an obligation we will be calling in one day."

"So no harm done?"

"I guess not." Alfieri paused, savouring a mental image that pleased him. "I want to see Emelia again. Same as last time. Same place. Arrange it. Next week. Wednesday or Thursday." He paused again, thinking. "And make sure Alessa's men have something to occupy themselves with."

Matteo could feel his resentment rising but showed no outward signs of disaffection. What his father had not thought to ask was: why was Zella talking with Alessa so much these days? He decided to keep that question to himself.

Chapter 21

Julia stepped out from Hotel Leonardo onto Borgo Pinti and opened the bright yellow hotel umbrella she'd taken from the stand near the exit. The late summer Tuscan heat had been broken by one of the sudden, intense showers that plagued the region.

The overhanging buildings sheltered the narrow street from the rain so you could walk the length of the street along the narrow pavement without getting wet. But you had to keep stepping off the pavement to let other pedestrians by and, once out on the equally narrow ribbon of the wet road, it was raining hard enough for a soaking.

She reached the gourmet restaurant near the end of the street, gazing inside to observe the wealthy diners. Illuminated by candlelight, enjoying the exotic food, laughing, telling stories; a world apart from her now troubled existence.

There was no sign of Giuseppe following. She was alone.

She'd planned to meet Anna at the restaurant in Piazza di San Pier Maggiore but at the last minute Anna had cancelled. Still, Julia needed to eat. She'd decided to dine alone.

The drunks had been cleared from outside the gourmet restaurant. They'd moved to the short covered passageway connecting the end of Borgo Pinti with Piazza di San Pier Maggiore to shelter from the rain and as she approached she could begin to make out their silhouetted forms.

Crossing the busy Via delle Badesse, she entered the passageway. There they were. More agitated now in the latter part of the day; the morning's alcohol and its warming sense of wellbeing pointing now to a colder, harsher place that inspired suspicion and anger. Their agitated movements seemed to be serving little purpose other than to introduce a sense of near panic to all around. One man was loudly complaining about something none of his companions seemed to care about.

She would have to walk past them.

She was better dressed for the encounter this time. No miniskirt. Instead, sensible trousers, a top coat against the rain. Nevertheless, as she approached they stopped arguing. She could feel the eyes taking in the shape of her body beneath her clothes.

There was a younger man with them this time; one who seemed particularly wired.

As she prepared to walk past them, Julia felt he would try to impede her but she kept her nerve and kept walking straight towards him. At the last minute he stood abruptly aside, a reward for her courage. As she passed, the agitation and loud argumentation resumed behind her.

Just a short walk to the restaurant. They were serving at the tables outside despite the rain but she preferred the relative safety of the inside restaurant. She asked for a table for one, was greeted with a smile and shown to the area at the back of the restaurant, beside the centrepiece, the large wood-burning oven they used to bake pizza.

It was then that her life changed. There would be no going back, no retracing of time and space, no logic that could be applied to change this moment.

There, seated at one of the tables facing the one she'd been offered, sat a couple, a handsome man and his girlfriend.

From her table, sitting beside Giancarlo, Emelia looked up as the well-dressed woman approached their table, intending to sit nearby. She gripped Giancarlo's arm. He looked from her to the woman who had just come in and the longer he looked the more incredulous his expression became.

They were one and the same. Emelia and this woman who had just walked in.

Julia stopped and for a long time could only stare. The first feeling was something close to horror. A doppelganger. A Cold War body-snatcher conspiracy, the outright fear of the Other. But this turned quickly to shock and then to surprise. And then to something else.

For Emelia there was the initial feeling of nightmare; she'd started hallucinating in some new and unforeseen side effect of the coke, she was losing her control of reality. But this passed when the woman who looked just like her came right up and gave her a huge embrace and, crying, began to kiss her.

For Julia, the feeling that had dogged her all her life, and that nothing, not even her love for Jim could alter, had a cause and a solution.

They embraced. They cried. They laughed. These two women who had never met but who knew so much about each other.

Part Three

Florence, four days later
Sunday August 31st to Tuesday September 2nd

Chapter 22

The trip via Paris had been stressful; the feeling that I was being tracked kept me all the time on guard and left me feeling exhausted, a feeling enhanced by the sudden jolt of heat as I stepped off the train onto the station concourse.

I queued to buy euros at the bureau de change just outside the busy tickets hall, turning half of my cash into the brightly coloured notes, and mingled with the Sunday afternoon crowds leaving the station, anonymous here amongst the tourists. Walking past the busy taxi rank, crossing the road with difficulty amidst the chaotic traffic, I headed for the Hotel Grande, a large unremarkable building not far from the station. The receptionist, a smart female Eastern European, had showed no surprise when I asked for a room for a week for cash with no prior reservation. The rate was not cheap; that must have been why they had vacant rooms. I had become just another tourist. The room was an imitation of an American chain hotel room, clean, serviceable, impersonal.

Following a short telephone call, I agreed to meet Sergio Romani.

It was Miles' doing. After trying his best to dissuade me from leaving London, he was at his best in suggesting

I would need the help of someone in Florence. He'd given me Sergio's number to call.

Sergio phoned again from the corridor outside the room so I was sure I should let him in.

"It's a pleasure to meet you," he said. He gave a warm smile, offering his hand. He was, young, bright-eyed, dressed casually for the heat in well-tailored light trousers and a designer checked shirt. Something in his demeanour gave a strong impression that he was the kind of man who knew more than enough about the ways of the world.

"So much like your brother," he said. "And, if I am not being too impolite, just as determined, I suspect."

I returned the handshake. "I've never seen Miles as the determined one. But to research all the stories he's published must have taken that, I'm sure."

"We have worked together, Miles and I, on and off for over four years. Miles as the writer, me as photographer. But the roles have come increasingly to overlap. Looking at corruption. Trying to uncover the networks involved in the illegal dumping of waste. It is international; Africa, South America, the States and, I am ashamed to say, it is here in Italy too."

"I don't want you to feel obligated to having to help me."

"Ah, the English reserve. Again, just like Miles. I know you are in trouble, Miles told me. But he didn't, or could not, tell me exactly what kind of trouble you are in. Whatever it is, I am here to help, whatever it takes."

"They've killed my wife."

"I am so sorry."

"She died in my arms, in our apartment in London. I'm trying to find the killers."

"In Florence?"

"She was here working as a conservator, working on paintings."

"Then Florence is the place to be."

"I have her pocket drive. She'd found a way of updating it from here, I think. The files are encrypted. But I'm finding ways of guessing the passwords she used to protect them."

"File synchronisation; I use it myself." Sergio looked pleased to be able to display his technical knowledge. "Useful for keeping my home computer updated from wherever I am travelling on an assignment. The software is readily available."

"Even remotely, say between Florence and London?" I asked.

"Of course," Sergio said. "Just as long as the home computer is connected to the Internet. And you can select a backup drive and assign the encryption to files to be sent to it from wherever you are. But why would she want to encrypt her files?"

"I think she was in dispute with the boss of the conservation studio where she worked. I think it was a way of preventing him from stealing her ideas."

"Rivalry between colleagues can be intense in any walk of life."

"I know. Julia was working on the idea that she could find a lost masterpiece using her conservation skills. If she succeeded there could be a great deal of prestige – and money – involved."

"And you do not know if she'd succeeded?"

"No. I blame myself. Too concerned with my own work to follow what she'd been doing."

Sergio placed a consoling hand on my shoulder in a way that seemed so natural we might have known each other for much longer. "I understand. It is what modern life has become for us all."

"I didn't want this to turn into a confessional. She also sent me this message." I showed Sergio the picture of *Leda and the Swan* on the phone. "She may have been looking for this."

"Ah, the Michelangelo." Sergio sighed. "A great treasure."

"A great lost treasure," I said. "And there was this message: *help me.*"

"She was in trouble?"

I nodded.

I realised, as I briefed Sergio, just how little I really knew about Julia's death and the thought shocked me.

"Now, those files, the ones on your wife's drive…"

"Julia."

"Yes, the ones on Julia's drive. You haven't been able to open them?"

"Nothing yet. But I'm sure I'm going to get there."

"If I can help, just let me know."

I thanked him. "Oh," I said in an as matter-of-fact manner as possible, "the police back in Britain think I did it. And two guys followed me in London and tried to kill me."

Sergio was unfazed. "And the English police, they know you are here?"

"I had to show my passport on leaving the UK and on arrival in Paris. It might not take too much deduction to work out I was heading for Florence. The hotel asked to see my passport when I checked in and I guess they report such things to some government department somewhere here. If the English police care to ask, I suppose they can find out pretty quickly where I am. But for the time being, I'm just another tourist."

"The Ministry of the Interior is not known for its rapidity in such situations," Sergio said. "But even they could find you very easily. I would say you have only limited time to play with."

"That will depend on just how keen Hendricks and his men are on fitting me up."

"Hendricks?"

"He's the officer in charge in London."

"I'll keep an eye out through my contacts for any requests made about you. We need to make the most of what we hope is our few days head start."

Sergio could see I was tired after the journey.

He said farewell and left me alone in the room.

Chapter 23

Setting up the laptop, I connected Julia's pocket drive. It took some time to master the hotel's Wi-Fi system but soon I was connected to the Internet and free to get back to the problem of discovering what Julia had been doing in the last few days of her life.

Frustration was immediate as I called up icons of files that would not open because I lacked the correct encryption password.

It couldn't be that difficult, surely. Julia had shared so much; I must know enough to start to work this out.

I tried to think about everything and anything Julia might have said to me about the information she kept on her computer. Anything that might offer a clue. Other people used birthdays or where they lived to set up passwords but I knew Julia would have wanted something less easy to guess than that. Again, if she was not going to make another of the most common mistakes and write the password down, it would have to be something she would be able to remember easily. Then, I remembered the time we'd been out for a meal at a Turkish restaurant near the Globe Theatre on the South Bank and had returned to the apartment feeling tipsy and I'd been teasing her about being such a geek over her computer. I'd jokingly boasted that I could get to her passwords in just twenty questions if she could answer only 'yes' or 'no' to them. She'd won and I'd been unable to guess the answer.

We'd laughed and gone off to bed to make love and I hadn't thought again about this until now. Those twenty questions with her 'yes' or 'no' answers must have taken me close. I struggled to recall every word she'd said that night, nine months ago. One remembered fact emerged. Julia had been using the names of places in the Lake District, where we'd spent our honeymoon and which, as a favourite place, we returned to as often as we could. As far as I could now recall, that was as far as the game had gone.

I called up maps of Cumbria from the browser and started to think of the names of the places we'd visited: Braithwaite, Greystoke, Birkrigg, Applethwaite, Hawkshead, Pooley Bridge, Shoulthwaite, Troutbeck... I started typing in the names into the dialogue boxes that popped up requesting the password each time I tried to open one of Julia's encrypted files. A sensible intuition, but not a correct one. The files refused to open.

I thought it through again. Julia would know that more than this was needed to create a password that would not be easily guessed by de-encryption software. So, she would have gone further. If I was right and the places we knew were part of the password, was there a second piece of information she'd added? Something personal; something easy for her to remember but not obvious to anyone else. I realised that back in the twenty questions game I'd deduced she'd been combining two pieces of information, one possibly a date, to make up the passwords. I struggled to recall the exact details of what we'd said all those months ago. That's right, Julia had also answered 'yes' to my question about whether she ever used the date we'd got married. That was 10th August 2005. It would come out as 100805.

I typed the date into the dialogue box and it was not accepted. Yet Julia had said I'd got close with the twenty questions. So maybe, I thought, it was all about the combination of the place names and the date.

I typed in Shoulthwaite100805 into each of the open dialogue boxes on the laptop screen that were calling for a password. None was accepted. I did the same with each of the place names and still nothing gave. I typed in 100805Shoulthwaite into each of the open dialogue boxes reversing the order of our wedding date and the place name and tried this with each of the place names and still none was accepted. I was tiring further and feeling more and more that I was not looking in the right direction. Still, some dogged persistence forced me to continue, the same kind of determination I'd developed as a youngster in Birmingham. I started to shuffle the numbers and place names into each other. 10Shoo8ulto5hwaite.

10Shou081thwo5aite.

One of the files opened.

A folder full of e-mails.

The same code didn't work on the remaining files. She'd chosen a different password for each file. But this was a start, a proof that I could succeed in retracing Julia's steps.

I lay back on the bed. "Screw you Hendricks. And your team of consultants."

It would take time and a little luck but eventually I knew it would be possible to access the information on Julia's drive.

Reading through the material in the first file I'd managed to open, it was clear that nearly all the messages related to Julia's work at the Clinton Ridley Conservation Studio. Ridley himself, the founder of the studio, featured in many of the messages. At first he appeared as a mentor, encouraging Julia in her quest to find a hidden masterpiece. But later, he featured more as an impediment to her progress, raising niggling objections and then as an outright enemy, seeking to limit Julia's field of action, raising objections to what she planned to do.

There was evidence, discussed in further messages with colleagues in the studio, including Myra, that in the past Ridley had been ruthless in claiming the sole credit and financial benefit for work they had in fact produced as a team. Julia had started to object, the messages exchanged with Ridley becoming terse and even threatening.

At least one thing was now understood, I thought. The reason why Julia had encrypted the information on her computer was clear. It was to prevent Ridley from stealing her best ideas and benefiting from them.

I phoned Sergio who picked up immediately.

"I've had some success."

"With all of the files?"

"No, just one folder containing about a hundred or so e-mails, exclusively stuff from work, mainly between the studio head, Clinton Ridley, Julia and Myra McKenzie, her colleague, about the conservation activity and a little about Julia's planning for her trip to Florence."

"Have you found any names of people here in Florence?"

"There don't seem to be any messages in the folder addressed to people in Florence, but there are one or two names mentioned in passing in the internal messages that could refer to people here. One is Anna Pini. Julia must have been planning to meet her. I think she must be a fellow conservator."

"I don't know the name," Sergio said. "It's not so surprising, there are many hundreds of conservators in this town. I'll make enquiries. Anyone else?"

"A woman called Alessa. Alessa Lando."

Sergio's voice quieted to a whisper. "Then, I have to tell you that the thought of the police catching up with you may be the smallest of your worries. The Landos are one of the oldest and most notorious families in Tuscany. They are involved in just about every crooked deal in the region – money laundering, protection, racketeering, drugs, prostitution. Many people in the Florence area know they are involved but no one will speak out."

"What on earth was Julia doing working with a woman like that?"

Sergio changed the subject. "I will try to locate Anna Pini. When I do I will call you."

I wanted to ask him more but ended the call as sleep descended upon me.

Chapter 24

The next morning was spent in a bind. So long as no one knew I was here in Florence it would be relatively safe. And this meant not only the police but also the Landos. But I would never be able to get close to the evidence that could lead to Julia's killer if I was unable to track it down. And every moment spent in hiding meant time was favouring Hendricks and his men in closing in. It would only be possible to break the bind by taking risks.

I had breakfast brought to the hotel room and spent more time seeking to open the remaining files on Julia's drive. Perhaps I could make some progress there. The old frustrations returned as I repeatedly entered variants on Lake District place names and reordered versions of our wedding date. In two hours, I'd opened just one more folder. It contained a listing of paintings and, in most cases, an image of each one; it was the inventory of lost masterpieces that Julia was using as a basis for her search. I read through the first part of the list:

School of Fra Angelico Last Judgment (1456) – believed to have been lost in fire, Berlin, May 1945

Sandro Botticelli Various Lagan paintings (1470-1490) – destroyed in the Bonfire of the Vanities, Florence, 1497

Sandro Botticelli Portrait of Cosimo De' Medici (1478) – believed to have been destroyed in World War II

Giovanni Bellini The Supper at Emmaus (1494) – believed to have been destroyed by fire, Vienna, 18th century

Ghirlandaio Jerome and John the Baptist (1496) believed to have been destroyed by fire, Berlin, May 1945

Fra Bartolomeo Assumption of the Virgin (1508) – believed to have been destroyed by fire, Berlin, May 1945

Leonardo da Vinci Leda and the Swan (1508) – lost, location unknown

Michelangelo Leda and the Swan (1530) – lost in the 16th Century, location unknown

Raphael Portrait of a Young Man - lost in World War II, location unknown

Titian Doge Gritti Praying to the Virgin – lost in a fire in the Doge's Palace, Venice, 1577

Tintoretto Last judgment – lost in a fire in the Doge's Palace, Venice, 1577...

There were further details of lost paintings from later years but my attention rested on the image of Michelangelo's *Leda and the Swan*. Why from this whole list had Julia sent me just this one image? Perhaps, despite the scepticism of her colleagues at the conservation studio, she'd found it. If true, was this a motivation for her death? Any one of these paintings would be worth in excess of fifty million. Many people had died for a whole lot less.

From all I could see in the files in the folder, there was no way of knowing if Julia had found the missing *Leda* or not. I had to admit the chance of finding any one of these missing pictures was small, despite Julia's knowledge of the subject and the sophisticated techniques of analysis she had available.

I was thinking this through when the mobile phone started beeping.

"I hope you are safe and well," Sergio said as soon as I accepted the call. "I've made a little progress."

"It's good to hear from you, Sergio. I've been cooped up in the hotel room, searching through Julia's files. Guess what? I've opened another of her folders."

"Anything useful?"

"I didn't think so at first. There's only one file and it's a list of 15th and 16th century paintings that have been lost or destroyed. Of course, the Michelangelo *Leda* is in the list, but there's a whole wealth of other material by Botticelli, Leonardo, Caravaggio, Raphael, Titian, Tintoretto."

"Any one of those paintings would be worth many millions," Sergio said.

"Many of them are believed to have gone missing in Berlin in 1945."

"That's because of Hitler's plan to set up a Fuhrer Museum in his home town of Linz in Austria. He had special units systematically stealing art works from the countries overrun in World War II. They took more than twenty-three thousand art works from France alone. Many more from Russia. Most were shipped to Berlin – by the train-full. Many have still not been recovered."

"So maybe this explains Julia's determination to find a missing masterpiece; there are so many of them out there."

"But I don't think the Nazi connection will help us. Julia sent you a picture of the Michelangelo. It has been missing for over four hundred years. Why did she send you that? This has to be our question."

"I still don't know." I fell silent.

"Anyway, I have some news," Sergio said. "Julia's contact in the conservation world in Florence, Anna Pini. I have found her. She works in the Bargello. She has agreed to meet me in an hour's time at your hotel."

"That's fine. See you then." I was about to close down the call when Sergio insisted on continuing.

"One more thing. Something you said about two men following you and trying to kill you."

"You don't believe me."

"No. It's not that." Sergio paused. "It's more the possibility this piece of knowledge might be one of the most important we have. Why would someone want to kill you? Find the answer to this and we may have important leads on what happened to Julia."

Chapter 25

It took fewer than five minutes to tell Anna what had happened.

She was in a state of shock after she'd heard what I had to say. "You mean Julia is dead?"

We'd met, as arranged, at 3.00 PM in the bar at the hotel. Sergio took the lead in making the introductions. Anna's delight and interest in meeting Julia's husband had turned to dismay when she'd heard the terrible news.

Anna was sobbing. "I did try to warn her. When I heard she was working with the Lando family, I knew she could be in danger."

"But she wasn't worried by what you had to say?"

"She promised to be careful. That's the only answer I could get out of her. She only seemed to care about getting a good source of paintings for her project and the Landos had in their collection just the kind of pictures she was looking for. She didn't seem to care when I told her they were a notorious crime family."

"Do you know how far she got in working with them?"

"I know she planned to meet Alessa Lando to discuss scanning the pictures in her house near Lucca. Julia seemed so pleased she'd managed to negotiate the deal to do this. I didn't see much of her after our meeting at the Bargello last week. I assumed she was busy scanning the paintings."

"Right now, we need all the information you can recall about what she was saying about her plans. Anything you can remember, no matter how trivial it might seem."

"And what are you going to do?" Anna asked. "If the Landos were involved in any way in Julia's killing, the best thing you could do is to go to the police. Even then, you'd need protection. There's a list of people who have crossed them and have never been heard of again."

Sergio nodded. "You're right. Everyone knows it, but no one does anything about it."

"I don't think Julia told me anything more."

"Perhaps not right now," I said. "Give it some time. Something might occur."

A grey-haired man with a full but neatly-trimmed beard walked through the hotel lobby and, seeing Anna, came over to introduce himself.

"Dr Pini," he said, offering his hand to her, ignoring both me and Sergio as if he hadn't seen us. "Clinton Ridley of the Clinton Ridley Restoration Studio, Mayfair. I hope I'm not interrupting."

"Do I know you?" Anna asked him.

"I'm a colleague of Julia Blake's. I met you with her at last year's restoration conference in Trieste, as I recall." He spoke with a mannered intonation that matched the cliched nature of his dress – brown corduroy suit, yellow red-spotted bow tie, highly polished brown brogue shoes; taken together with the grey hair and beard, everyone's idea of the art connoisseur.

"Of course," Anna said. "But this is not a good time to talk of Julia. Have you heard?"

"That's one of the reasons why I'm here," Ridley said. "Shocking tragedy; we're all distraught at the studio, I can assure you. But our business has to go on. Julia had invested a considerable amount of time and money in projects here in Florence; I'm here to try to pick up the pieces of her work, particularly with the university."

Ridley had still not noticed me, nor paid any attention to Sergio.

So here was the man of whom Julia was so suspicious, the man who had led her to encrypt her files. Too much of a coincidence that he'd turned up in Florence and at the same hotel.

I gave Anna a look that said: *go ahead and tell him*.

"Dr Ridley."

"The name's Clinton, remember?"

"Clinton." She looked over at me. "You need to meet James Blake."

"My good man," Ridley said. He turned to me and offered his hand. "I had no idea you were here. I'm sorry I didn't recognise you. It must be a terrible time for you, trying to come to terms with what has happened to our poor Julia."

I was so angry at the man's hypocrisy that I was finding it difficult to contain myself. But control myself I must. "I've heard so much about you from Julia."

Ridley interrupted. "Mostly positive I hope."

"It's a pity we couldn't have met under better circumstances," I said. "What happened to Julia is something I think I'll never really come to terms with. But coming here, getting a feel for the kind of work she was doing is something that in the long term may help. This is the only way I can think of it right now."

"Allow time to pass. It won't get any easier but the bleak perspective will eventually change, trust me."

I introduced Sergio as a friend of Anna's. Anna, still distressed, didn't seem to mind.

"So, what do we know about how far Julia had got with her work here?" Ridley asked. His calculated indifference was aimed at us all.

"We're mostly in the dark," I said. "She's been quite secretive and I must admit I haven't spent enough time paying attention to her, let alone her work."

"We've got nothing at the studio," Ridley said. "The police have taken away her computer and there don't seem to be any backups left in her office. Rather strange, don't you think, that she's kept so much of this work secret from her employer? She must have confided in someone." He seemed to be accusing both Anna and me at the same time.

I was thinking: the time would come when it would be right to test Ridley on what he knew about the Michelangelo, but not yet. Time was needed to work out exactly what he was doing in Florence.

"If there is anything you'd care to share with me, let me know." With that Ridley stood and prepared to go. "I'm in room 623. Give me a call. I'm sure we can help each other."

"Now, that was difficult," I said, as soon as Ridley was out of earshot. "Why do I get the feeling he's already formed the opinion we're holding out on him?"

"I guess he suspects Julia may have given him a bad press with all of us," Anna said. "Maybe he is just testing us out."

"What I might have told him, if I felt I could trust him more," I said, "was that Julia was almost certainly looking for something specific that she wanted no one to know about under one of those Lando paintings – *Leda and the Swan*, the Michelangelo. Julia sent me a picture of it on my mobile phone."

"Everyone in the conservation business knew she was looking for just such a painting. It would be a sensation. To rediscover such a painting after all these years. How wonderful it would be." In another context, Anna might have sounded excited, but in her state of despair at the news about Julia, this came over as little more than a disinterested observation.

"Either way, it is essential to keep this secret," I said. "It could offer the best chance of finding Julia's killers."

Anna nodded solemnly, indicating the importance of what she'd been told. She looked up, clearly remembering something. "Julia was staying at a hotel in Borgo Pinti, the Leonardo, I'm sure that is its name."

Chapter 26

The manager at the reception at the Hotel Leonardo was polite but disengaged. I'd made my way there through the heat of the day on foot, weaving around the crowds waiting for admittance to the Duomo and then on through the shop-lined streets along the busy Via dell'Oriuolo until I'd come to the narrow entrance to Borgo Pinti where, with a further short walk halfway along the narrow street, I'd found the hotel.

When I asked about Julia after giving my name, the manager looked concerned. "Signora Blake. She checked out."

"But did she say anything about her future plans?"

"Signor Blake. Even for a husband, we respect the privacy of our guests. So even if she'd taken us into her confidence, I would not be at liberty to tell. But I can assure you, she didn't in any case leave any word about her plans."

"This is not about a tiff between husband and wife," I said. "I have to tell you the reason I'm here is that my wife, Signora Blake, has been killed, murdered in London."

The manager looked shocked, his noncommittal manner slipping, if only for a moment. If someone had told him to keep quiet they hadn't told him the gravity of the information he was being asked to cover up.

"All I know is she was staying here," I continued. "Something must have happened to make her leave for London, a series of events that led to her death on that Friday afternoon."

"The register clearly shows that Signora Blake checked out of Hotel Leonardo on Friday 29th August. I was not on duty myself. But the time is clearly stated as 9:30 AM, Friday morning. What are you asking of us?"

"I need you to tell me if she gave any indication of why she was going. She was not expected to leave for at least another week."

"She decided to check out. She gave no reason. As I said, even for a husband we could not say, even if we knew."

"Could I talk to the person who was on duty when my wife checked out?"

"I don't think that is going to be necessary," the manager said. "I'm seriously thinking of calling the police. I'm offended that you would choose to invent such a lie about your wife in order to try to extract information it is our policy not to give. This is something they will be very interested in at the Questura, I am sure."

The prospect of the police was daunting. The manager knew that, or had sensed it. I knew I would get nowhere if the police picked me up and put me back into the hands of Hendricks.

"You must understand," I said. "All I have told you is true. I can assure you."

"I'm sure in the end you will find her." The manager's cynicism was clear.

"I'd like to see the room my wife stayed in. It would help me get a perspective on the time she spent here."

The manager looked at me with pity, criticising me with a look for wanting to maintain the pretence that I was in mourning for Julia. "There's no harm in it," he said at last. "The room is not occupied at the moment; it's nothing we would not willingly do for any prospective guest." He shouted to an assistant in the back office: "Avellina! Will you please show this gentleman to room 311."

A pert Russian girl in a black suit emerged, smiled, took the keys to the room from the rack behind the reception desk and showed me to the ground floor lift. I didn't know what to expect from the visit to the room. It didn't matter that the manager would not believe me; the undeniable impulse was to find any connection to Julia; to find a way of reaching out to her. Even though the room would have been cleaned since Julia had been there, I hoped some trace of her might remain.

It was a splendid room in the Italian formal style with shuttered windows and a red stone floor to militate against summer heat, thick brocade wallpaper and a high ceiling with heavily embossed features in the ornate plasterwork. In the centre, there was a double bed with more brocade in the bedspread and in the scatter cushions built up in a pile on top of the pillows. At each side of the bed was the expected bedside cabinet. Against the facing wall, a large antique wardrobe with mirrored doors and drawers beneath completed the room.

"Each room is cleaned after each guest has left," the Russian girl said in broken English. "Nothing remains."

"I know. It's more to get a feel for where my wife spent the last days of her life."

The girl showed little remorse. She said coldly, "I will wait outside."

Alone in the room, I checked over the small bathroom. There was nothing there; as expected it had been depersonalised and restocked with the hotel's own label shampoo and shower gel.

I quickly searched the bedside cabinets, finding only the Gideon Bible. I leafed through its pages, hoping that concealed there might be something to link me to whatever had happened to Julia in the last days of her life. But the bible was empty, as empty as my heart at that moment.

I searched the wardrobe and the rest of the room and found nothing.

When the Russian girl returned, I pretended I was lost in contemplation. "It is a help to visualise her being here," I said. The girl offered a reassuring but unbelieving smile.

Returning to the lobby, I acknowledged the manager and headed for the hotel exit. The manager nodded back indifferently.

Leaving the hotel and walking back along Borgo Pinti, I noticed that two cars were approaching from behind. I stood aside on the narrow pavement to allow the vehicles to pass but only one of them did so, the other remaining behind me. The car that had passed me stopped. The front doors were opened, touching the buildings on both sides of the narrow street, blocking the way ahead. Behind me the second car had also stopped and the front doors had been opened in a similar fashion, removing any possibility of retreat. I was trapped.

During the time I'd spent in Julia's room, the manager must have made a phone call. He must have been complicit after all.

A burly man dressed in jeans and a T-shirt who was at least twice my weight emerged from the leading car and casually withdrew a gun from his waistband. He motioned me to get into the rear passenger seat. There was nothing to do but to get into the car. The doors closed. Both vehicles resumed their journey.

It was broad daylight on a Monday afternoon in central Florence. I'd been abducted and no one had seen a thing.

Chapter 27

As the kidnap car sped through the narrow streets in the direction of the Arno, my possessions were expertly searched by the large T-shirted man who had captured me on Borgo Pinti. With the gun trained on me, I was gestured to give up my wallet and mobile phone. The wallet was quickly checked for anything incriminating and handed back. He had no interest in the cash it held. The sim card and battery were removed from my phone. Instructed to hold my arms away from my sides, I was frisked to make sure I was not carrying a wire or a weapon. Everything that was happening suggested I was in the hands of men who had done this many times before.

In addition to the large man on the back seat beside me, there were two others; the driver, a balding man with a poor, blotchy appearance with flakes of skin visible on the open collar of his orange shirt, and a younger man dressed incongruously for the heat of the day in a dark formal suit.

I heard one of them call the younger man "Matteo" and was sure it was he who was in control.

As we drew closer to the Arno, a long, white crepe bandage was produced and wrapped round my head, covering my eyes. The intention, it seemed, was to make out they were doing no more than helping a colleague who had been involved in some kind of accident. At the same time, I would not know where I was being taken.

In just a few minutes they'd rendered me depersonalised and sightless. I'd never felt so frightened as I realised they could do anything with me they wished.

The car stopped at a place I took to be somewhere close to the river. I was led from the car in the manner in which an invalid is caringly helped. There was a walk up a short flight of steps, through a doorway, along a long corridor, through another doorway and into a larger, echoing room. I was seated on a chair and the bandage was removed.

I was sitting in a room of considerable opulence and little taste. Carrera marble had been used almost everywhere with no expense spared. There were gold fittings embedded in the marble used to manufacture tables, shelving and chairs.

The man facing me stared at me with an undiluted intensity. He had the look of a killer who had gone up in the world and had adopted the well-fed, well-groomed, stylishly-clothed patina of the wealthy post middle-aged Italian but who would remain a killer nonetheless.

"My name is Alfieri Lando, Signor Blake. I believe you do not know me, but let me assure you, I know more than enough about you."

"Then you have me at a further disadvantage." I was still straining to adjust my vision now the bandage had been removed. "I would have thought kidnapping me and bringing me here like this was disadvantage enough."

"My son, Matteo, can be heavy-handed at times, I know," Lando said. "But because of who you are and what you have been doing, what else would you expect?"

"Then tell me. Why have you brought me here?"

"Sometimes, Signor Blake, someone places themselves, or gets placed, at a point that is at one and the same time a danger to others and quite impossible to have been arrived at by chance."

"I've no idea what you mean."

"Look at it this way – your brother, Miles, is an investigative journalist seeking to damage Italian business by making false claims that we do not dispose of our waste properly. He has teamed up with a photographer here in Florence. Your wife, Julia, appears here on the pretence of making an arrangement with my wife to do work on her paintings. And now you are here, asking questions. It should not be too difficult to understand why I need to take an interest in you."

My thoughts were racing. I was trying to understand how Lando already knew so much about me. "You have to believe me. I have one reason and one reason only for being here in Florence. That concerns the death of my wife, Julia. I'm here to discover how her death came about."

Lando did not show surprise. He was too shrewd and worldly-wise for that. Lando then raised his eyes and said casually, "And the manner of her death?"

"By assassination," I said. "A tampered-with bullet in the back of the head in our own home in London." I was becoming less and less surprised to hear the words.

"You have my sincerest condolences," Lando said without irony. "That is no way for a woman to die. But as I told you, Signor Blake, the world does not run on coincidence. If your wife did not have a husband whose brother was prying into our affairs, perhaps I could believe differently."

"I didn't know this. I did not know my brother Miles was involved with your family in any way."

"Don't you understand why I am having great difficulty in believing you?" Lando's sharp eyes looked upward.

"It's the truth. Miles has not told me anything about his work. I know he is an investigative reporter, of course. But he's not been confiding in me. I had no idea he was interested in you or your family. As far as I know he's been working on a story in the United States."

I tried to move on the conversation as quickly as possible. "I can prove to you my wife was here genuinely to look at paintings. Clinton Ridley, the owner of the conservation studio she works for, is here in Florence. He can explain exactly what she was doing."

"I don't know why, Signor Blake, but I am inclined to listen to you. We will be in contact with Signor Ridley. If he is involved as you say, it is important that I understand what he knows and what his intentions are."

He paused and looked towards the right hand corner of the room. It was only then I realised that the dark-suited man who had led the kidnapping had been sitting listening. "And remember, Signor Blake, that it will not be difficult for Matteo to find you and bring you here again."

"And don't think the police will be of any help," Matteo said. "That would be foolish."

"That is all," Lando said.

Matteo was now standing behind me and had already begun to wind the crepe bandage around my head as Alfieri Lando stood and walked out of the room.

I was led back the way I'd come to a waiting car that set off in the direction of the Duomo. Once again I'd become an unfortunate casualty of some unknown accident and was being helped by my caring colleagues, observed by and remarked on by no one.

As I was bundled out of the car, Matteo gave me back my phone. Fifteen minutes after leaving the Lando building, I was released at the exact same place on Borgo Pinti where I'd been captured. The bandage removed, I shook my head, trying to clear my vision as the car pulled away.

I'd lost an hour of my life.

I resumed the walk along the narrow street, heading back towards my hotel as I'd intended an hour before.

Chapter 28

As soon as the air conditioning in the hotel room kicked in and cooled me down, I called Sergio and told him it was imperative to meet as soon as possible. He agreed to come to the hotel room and within half an hour he was there, knocking on the door.

I opened the door after checking through the spy hole that it was him. "Come in. We have something to talk about."

"I haven't made much progress in my enquiries on your behalf," Sergio said.

"They took me off the street."

"Who?"

"The Landos. Alfieri and his son Matteo. They bundled me into a car in broad daylight."

"Took you where?"

"To Lando's place. Somewhere down by the Arno. But I don't know where. I was blindfolded."

Sergio looked concerned. "And you met Alfieri Lando?"

"I wouldn't say 'met'. More summoned into his presence."

"I did try to warn you."

"Let's get real here," I said. "You haven't been straight with me, have you? It nearly just cost me my life. Those bastards could have done anything they wanted with me. No one would have known."

"I'm sorry."

"You knew all along that Miles was investigating the Landos and you were helping him. The illegal dumping story. Had you both become so involved you couldn't see anything else?"

He looked down. "We've been working on it on and off for over three years. I thought of telling you. But more than once the Landos have managed to slip out of our grasp just at the point where we thought we were about to nail them."

"So you decided not to tell me?"

"It was a decision we took. Miles and myself made each other promise there were no circumstances under which we could jeopardise the investigation by bringing others into the equation."

"Not even a brother?"

"That was the dilemma for Miles. If it helps, I know he felt terrible not being able to tell you."

I was angry and I could feel that anger rising to a level I would hardly be able to control. "So you endangered me to protect your story?"

Sergio sat in silence; not denying what had been said.

"Those two men following me in London. The ones trying to kill me. You knew all about them, didn't you?"

"We could not be sure."

"But you had a strong enough idea to tell me they might be key to my uncovering the cause of Julia's death. The reason why they were following me was because of Miles, wasn't it?"

"You met him and they must have been watching," Sergio said. "They may have thought he'd handed you something, that you are part of the investigation."

"Enough for them to want to kill me?"

"We do not know for sure. Anyone who was a contact of Miles' could potentially have been seen by them as a problem. It was something out of our control."

The full dimension of the damage the secrecy over the investigation had caused was suddenly becoming clear.

"You may have endangered Julia," I said. "Your investigation may have been the reason she was killed!"

"I don't see how you can say that."

"I've just been told by Alfieri Lando how suspicious she looked to them. Here in Florence, looking at the family paintings, too much of a coincidence for them to swallow."

"Not a coincidence," Sergio said. He looked guiltier than ever.

"Tell me!" I was shouting, struggling to control the anger coming now in strong waves.

"It was Miles," Sergio said, his voice a whisper. "He suggested it to Julia. That the Landos had a collection of paintings of just the right type for her project."

"And he hoped to somehow use her to get information on the Landos?"

"We needed to know about their security systems, that's all," Sergio said. "Miles may have planned to get that information from Julia when the time was right. I can't be sure. There seemed to be something else leading Miles to make the recommendation but he didn't confide in me about it."

"But, she didn't know… about the investigation?"

"Miles thought it would be safer that way. If she didn't know there would be nothing for her to betray."

"That's unforgivable. To place an innocent woman in danger just to advance your story."

"You can see how ashamed I am," Sergio said. "If we could go back we would do this differently."

"What you don't get, Sergio, is that a woman, my wife, has died and there is no going back. If I felt it might make any difference, I would kill you, right here and now. As it is, I need you to help me find her killers."

Sergio looked frightened, shocked by my threat. "I have already taken a great risk in making contact with you," he said. "Everything I have been able to do here in Florence has depended on my identity being secret. If the Landos knew where I was, they would kill me. I am trying in some small way to make amends."

"So, be straight with me. Where is Miles? When I tried to call him there was no reply."

"He's only just arrived in the States, checking on the Lando's operations there."

"Get him for me. Now."

"I am only to call him in emergency," Sergio said.

"This is an emergency. Call him!"

Sergio thought of protesting further, but could see from my eyes he had no choice but to make the call. Within a minute he'd made connection to Miles' phone.

"It's James," he said as he handed me the phone.

"Brother, what can I do to help?" Miles said.

"You could tell me why you endangered me and how your recklessness involved Julia, too!" I shouted. "I *know*, Miles. Why couldn't you have confided in me?"

"Know what?"

"You set up Julia. You put her life in danger. You didn't even let her know she was at risk. You got her killed. And you are no brother of mine."

I hit the end call button and returned my gaze to Sergio. "I want you to go now."

Chapter 29

Not long after Sergio had left, there was a call from the hotel manager asking if I would come to reception.

I'd been in a period of introspection in which I was following through all the events that had taken place since Julia was killed and the significance of the way the Landos had been able to pick me up so easily outside the Hotel Leonardo.

The ringing of the phone dragged me back to reality.

When I reached the reception desk, I was greeted with a smile and a gesture that suggested I should join the manager in the back office. A uniformed police officer was waiting, formal and proper in his grey and gold uniform, peaked cap folded under his arm, pistol clearly visible in its holster.

"Signor Blake. Signor James Blake?" he asked, looking at me with a disinterested gaze.

I nodded.

"You are to accompany me to the Questura," the officer said.

Sergio's contact had been of little help in warning me after all.

"May I ask what this is about?"

"Just come with me, Signor Blake. This is a request. If you refuse I am empowered to arrest you."

I was led out of the office via the hotel service exit. Waiting in the basement car park was the officer's Pantera, the Fiat coupe that the force patriotically provisioned. I was driven through the Florence streets to Via Zara in the north of the city, the silence broken periodically by the chatter of police messages on the in-car radio.

The Florence Questura, a grey stone building with an elegant entrance beneath a classical balcony sporting the Italian flag on a-five degree inclined flagpole, looked forbidding. The entrance hall was impressive by the standards I'd come to expect at home; a short flight of stone steps led up to a lobby area with polished wooden panelling at the end of which stood the sergeant's desk. Yet as I was ushered into the building, I couldn't help but be aware of the more sinister aspects of the Questura – the numerous barred windows facing out from the side of the building, no doubt the location of the interrogation rooms and the overnight cells where much of the real business of the place was carried out.

At the large mahogany desk at the end of the entrance hall, I was stood before the station sergeant whose long-suffering expression told more than words that there was nothing in the world he hadn't already seen.

"Signor James Blake." The arresting officer addressed the sergeant. "For Inspector Manieri."

The sergeant nodded and pressed a switch beneath the desk. A nearby door opened. I was led along a narrow passageway, up a flight on stairs and into an office marked *Chief of Questura – Inspector Bernardo Manieri*.

I was told to sit in a chair facing what must be Manieri's desk and to wait. My first thought as I sat alone in the room was they must be observing through hidden cameras, a ploy they probably used with every suspect brought into this office; give them time, make them feel nervous, soften them up. Before they'd even questioned me, I was feeling like a guilty man, working out how to respond to the questions I expected about where I was when the murder in London had been committed.

After a few minutes a door opened and a well-groomed middle-aged man dressed more like a politician than a police chief came in. Manieri, though dressed in a formal grey suit and wearing a military-looking tie, carried an air of approachability. He had a good reputation for fighting organised crime, and in doing as much as anyone could in slowing the drugs traffic in Tuscany. He gave no impression that working late at the Questura was anything unusual for him.

"Signor Blake." The Inspector sat behind the desk in a high-backed chair, facing me. "My name is Inspector Manieri. I apologise for the manner of your being brought here; it seemed best under the circumstances."

"I was about to come in," I said. "To report an incident."

"Yes?"

"An abduction. My abduction. I was taken off the street, in broad daylight. In a Florence street."

"And force was used?"

"Taken at gunpoint, against my will."

"Taken where?"

"I don't know. Somewhere down by the Arno. They blindfolded me."

"We have no reports of any incident of that kind. Did anyone see you?"

"They made it look as if I was being helped. Those who saw it, I don't think they would want to call the police."

"So who do you think is responsible?"

"They made no secret of it. The Landos. Alfieri and his son Matteo. They made no attempt to conceal their identities."

Manieri smiled. "They will deny it. It will be your word against theirs. We don't know where they took you, no one saw anything, and you are clearly unharmed. We would have no case to bring."

"They know that. It's how they continue to get away with kidnapping, like they get away with the rest of their shady business."

"Signor Blake," Manieri said. "Do not insult us. We know about the Landos. We know the kind of scum they are. I have half my men on the lookout for the slightest chance to move against them. But we have to have proof; it is the only currency. And they have lawyers in their pay who are expert in claiming that we, the police, are merely intimidating a respectable business family doing its best to better the prosperity of Italy. I'm sure you know about your Al Capone, Signor Blake. Everyone knew about the crimes he was committing; but in the end all that could be proven was tax evasion and that was what put him away."

"I'm sorry," I said. "I didn't want to imply you were somehow not pursuing them. I was shocked to be taken away by them in such a brazen way."

"We will investigate. Did they say why they took you?"

I told him about what had happened in London, about why I was here in Florence, looking for Julia's killers. "It was a warning not to ask too many questions."

His smile told me he already knew why I was here. "Why place yourself in danger, Signor Blake? You should leave this to the police."

I said nothing.

"It goes without saying, we will be keeping a closer eye on you in future. Now, to the reason for bringing you here."

Manieri picked up the phone and dialled the number he took from the diary that was open on the desk. There were short conversations with two intermediaries before Manieri handed the receiver to me. "For you," he said.

"Mr Blake, so good to make contact."

It was Hendricks. The shallow irony of his manner was all the more evident in his voice over the phone. "I hope you've been enjoying your time in Firenze?" He said the Italian name of the city with exaggeration, somehow implying there was something unsavoury in my being there.

"It's hard work being a tourist," I said. "August is not the best month. Too hot; too many mosquitoes, they can get you down."

"Yes, yes, Mr Blake. Very inconsiderate of you to leave London without telling us. Very foolish to think you would not be easy to find in Firenze. I could have you brought back as a material witness – or as a suspect."

I shuddered. "If you had enough to go on you wouldn't be saying that to me."

"I know that people like you, Mr Blake, don't think much of men like me. People with your education and your interest in the arts and such don't give much respect to someone who has had to work his way up from the beat."

"I don't know why you carry such a chip on your shoulder, Inspector Hendricks." I was aware that even if Hendricks had known about my own upbringing it would make no difference to the way he saw me. "What's wrong with social mobility?"

I could hear Hendricks' suppressed indignation at the comment. "Well, Mr Blake, you may be interested to know that men like me are good for something in your eyes."

I was having difficulty trying to work out where these comments were leading.

"The DNA matches," Hendricks said. "Your wife's DNA matched the DNA we took from the hair in the brush in the apartment. It also matched the DNA record we have of her when she was detained two years ago for a traffic offence. That's the database people like you say we should be destroying because it infringes people's civil liberties."

"Why are you telling me this again?" I asked.

"So the circle was complete." Hendricks continued without hearing me. "Except, I'm an old-fashioned copper. I like to see that the new ways match up to the expectations of the old ways. So I ran a fingerprint check, Mr Blake. Just out of the bloody-minded curiosity of an old copper who has worked his way up from the beat. We'd taken your wife's prints at the time of the same traffic incident. And you know what I found?"

"What, Inspector?"

"The prints do not match. The woman we found in your apartment is not your wife."

Chapter 30

I could feel myself falling into shock. What kind of cruel trick was Hendricks playing? The man knew I'd seen Julia die in my arms, had felt the last breath of life exit her body, had felt the anguish of the loss of the woman who meant everything to me. And Hendricks was seeking to play with all that, no doubt with some peculiar plan of trapping me into a confession. It was inhuman, and I responded.

"I don't know what you are trying to pull here, Hendricks, but it won't work. I'm not going to be drawn into your scheme to entrap me. She's dead; I saw her die. The DNA matches. What more do you want from me?"

"I checked the dental records," Hendricks said. "They don't match either. The woman who died is not your wife."

I was trying not to be taken in, yet I could feel belief growing inside. Julia was alive! She could be somewhere, waiting, hoping to be rescued.

"How can that be?" I asked.

"There is only one explanation," Hendricks said. "Same DNA; different fingerprints. It means only one thing. Your wife had an identical twin."

Inspector Manieri interrupted. He was listening to the conversation on the speakerphone. "Identical twins have the same DNA, in that sense they are inseparable. But no one, including twins, has the same fingerprints. They are unique to each individual."

I could feel my sense of disbelief weakening; feel the rush of optimism I'd sought so hard to suppress, rising. "And she is alive?"

"Put it this way," Hendricks said, "we have a body we've not been able to identify. Your wife is missing, and we don't know where she is. And that's all we know."

"I don't know where to begin," I said.

"You need to stay calm," Manieri said. "You need to allow time for this news to sink in."

"So tell me about the woman who died," Hendricks said. "You must know her."

I was expecting something like this from Hendricks. "You don't mean to say you still think I'm a suspect?"

"I never said you were a suspect, Mr Blake. Merely a material witness at this stage. Who was she?"

"I have no idea," I said. "You can't really think I've been pretending that my wife was dead all this time?"

"There you go again, Mr Blake," Hendricks said. "Always coming back with a question. Your involvement is something I can't rule out. There are some very devious people out there, people who would do anything to get away with murder."

"I'm not one of those."

"So I'd like to believe, Mr Blake. In the meantime you are, as I have stated, a witness material to the investigation of a murder. I could insist you return to London. Since I am sure you have no intention of doing that, I have asked Inspector Manieri to take care of you."

"We expect, and insist, Signor Blake, that you report here each day," Manieri said. "If you do not we will seek to return you to the care of our colleague in London. Is that understood?"

"Understood," I said.

"I'll put out a missing person's request for your wife, as I'm sure will Inspector Hendricks in London."

Manieri said his farewells to Hendricks and closed the phone line. "Good news, then, Signor Blake," he said without irony. "Oh, and Signor Blake, do not underestimate Inspector Hendricks. We have worked with him before. He is one of your most talented police officers."

I left the Questura having promised Manieri I would return the next day to go over all of the details of Julia's disappearance. And that I would get some rest.

Chapter 31

I travelled back to the hotel in a state of elation and remorse. Elation that Julia had not died in London. Remorse that I'd disowned my brother and jeopardised my relationship with Sergio. They had endangered her that was clear. But I knew I now needed their help all the more to attempt to find her.

I wanted to be back and to be able to act quickly but the car Inspector Manieri had arranged was delayed by traffic in the congested streets around the Duomo.

I gestured to the officer driving the Pantera. "I'll get out and walk."

The rear passenger door lock was released and I stepped out onto the crowded street and set off towards the hotel.

As I walked, I phoned Sergio and told him I wanted to speak to him again.

"I thought you would not want to see me ever again," Sergio said.

"I'm not apologising," I said. I was still feeling angry about how I'd been deceived by my brother and Sergio. "But something has happened. I need to see Miles."

"I phoned him again after you put the phone down on him. He was very upset."

I told Sergio what had taken place in Manieri's office. "What's changed," I said, "is that we now have to find Julia."

"Who was she?"

"The woman who died? I don't know, Sergio. I'm sure Julia was completely unaware she had a twin. They must have been separated at birth. She only told me that she'd been taken in by the Carpasian Sisterhood in Ireland and eventually given to the people in Guildford who became her parents. When she was thirteen they told her she was adopted but not that she was a twin."

"The Sisters playing God," Sergio said. "It would not be the first time."

"Would finding out more about that help to find Julia? It's the only thing that matters at the moment."

"The woman who died must have been in some sort of recent contact with Julia."

"Yes. And the clothes." I recalled the moment I'd held her in my arms, thinking she'd died. "She was dressed in Julia's clothes when I found her."

"Can you be sure of that?"

"As sure as anyone could be. They were the kind of clothes that she wore... that she wears."

"I'll try to convince Miles to come to Florence," Sergio said.

I was almost back at the hotel when he ended the call. I went straight to my room and set myself up at the small corner desk. I connected Julia's hard drive to my laptop and began again to deduce the passwords needed to open the remaining files contained on the disc. I resumed the task with a new energy, buoyed by the prospect that Julia could be found alive.

She'd been very methodical, as I knew she would. It was one of the things that made her so attractive. The clarity of thought that was such a complement to her beauty. I realised how much I longed to hear her voice once again, how much I wanted to feel her body against mine. And I felt the sorrow that someone else had died in order that I could feel this way again.

One by one, by shuffling the date of our marriage into the names of the places we'd visited during our times together in the Lakes, I succeeded in opening more of the fifty-three folders that Julia had created on the drive.

I spent over five hours reading the contents of Julia's meticulously ordered files. When I'd finished, I knew more about her visit to Florence, about scientific colleagues there, about the images she'd captured in the scanning of the Lando's paintings, about the continuing disagreement with Ridley. But at the end of it all, I had two images and two images only showing on the laptop screen.

They were tourist's snaps. The first showed two women sitting in a restaurant, arms linked, eyes sparkling, smiling, smiling, smiling. It was Julia and her murdered twin. The two women, Julia and her sister, were clearly identical yet there was no difficulty in telling them apart. Julia's sister had clearly lived the harder life. It wasn't just the cheaper clothes and the less subtle makeup that told them apart; there was a world of suffering in her sister's eyes that was unknown to Julia.

The second photograph showed the same two women but now joined by a young, elegant-looking man. He was seated between them with his arms round both. All three were smiling. Julia; the man; the murder victim. Arm in arm, smiling at the camera.

The reasons I had been seeking for Julia's murder were now the reasons for her disappearance and the chance to find her. The reasons why someone killed her sister were just as important to me, knowing as I did this could eventually lead to Julia.

I emailed the photographs to Sergio at the address he'd given me when we'd first met. I was prepared for a long wait but the reply came back almost immediately.

"I recognise the man. It is Giancarlo Orletti. He is with the Florence police, working undercover on the Lando case."

Back to the laptop, reading and re-reading Julia's files, aware that time was passing and I still hadn't found her.

I could feel my eyes closing. The day had come and gone. It had been one of the most taxing in my life.

Chapter 32

Next morning, after a troubled night's sleep, I presented myself early at the Questura, as requested. It was not yet nine o'clock when I arrived yet I was ushered straight into Inspector Manieri's office.

The appraisal of the requirements for the missing persons investigation was thorough and professional; Manieri asked probing questions on the details of Julia's visit to Florence that I answered to the best of my ability, my answers informed by my reading of Julia's files the night before. A uniformed police officer took notes as the interview proceeded.

"So the last you know of her whereabouts was she checked out of Hotel Leonardo at 9:30 AM on Friday," Manieri said.

"That's what the hotel manager says. I think he informed on me and got me abducted, as I told you."

"But that's the last time you can place your wife, she's not been in contact with you since?"

"Only once; by email. A message that was sent after she checked out of the hotel, the same day I found the body in the apartment in London."

I showed Manieri the message on my phone. He noted the time on the email header – 1.30 PM – and then took in the message – *help me.*

"It's what convinced me I should come here."

I called up the image of *Leda and the Swan.*

He frowned. "What do you take the painting to mean? Why do you think she sent you that?"

"I don't know. Just this image and a cry for help."

"And you think the message has a bearing on the death of the woman in the apartment in London?"

"Julia was looking for that painting, or others as valuable. Maybe there is a deeper connection."

Manieri was impressed by my attempt at impartiality. "Is there anything else you feel is material that you haven't already told us?" The inspector's tone suggested he was about to bring the interview to a close.

"Just this picture," I said.

I handed Manieri my phone once more. I'd copied the pictures I'd discovered in Julia's files. I was showing him the picture of Julia and her murdered twin seated in the restaurant.

"The two women together." Manieri looked carefully at the picture. "So we have proof they did meet before the woman's death."

"The date stamp on the picture puts that as just two days before the murder in London."

"Indeed," Manieri said. The intensity of his interest in the picture was sharpening. "Seeing the two women, side-by-side like this, the first sensation is how alike they are. They are identical, as you say in England. Your wife, educated and middle-class; the other woman, a woman living a hard life. And the more I look, Mr Blake, the more I realise we know her. Here at the Questura. The woman is known to us, I am sure."

"Grassi," he said to the uniformed officer who had been taking the notes, "get me Leonini from Squadra Mobile. Get him to come in."

The officer left and returned with the portly plain-clothes policeman, Leonini, just a few minutes later.

Manieri showed him the mobile phone picture with Julia's face covered by his thumb.

"Do we know her?"

"We do," Leonini said. "She is Emelia Rossellini; addict, high-class prostitute, linked to Matteo Lando. We've pulled her in for immorality and drug use many times. But overlooked the offences since she's not a pusher."

"Thank you," Manieri said. "You may go."

When Leonini had left, I said, "The other woman, Emelia Rossellini, the woman who died in London."

"Yes, it must be her."

"There's a strong connection to the Landos once again. Surely, you have to move against them."

"With what evidence?"

"Julia was involved with them, scanning the paintings."

"That's not going to be enough. I will question Alessa Lando. She will deny knowledge of anything but the involvement in the paintings. I have no grounds for questioning Alfieri or Matteo Lando."

"Isn't it your duty to find my wife?"

"We will be doing all that is necessary," Manieri said. "Report here as usual tomorrow and I will give you an update. And do not interfere in police business." He took a note of my phone number. "So I can contact you,

Signor Blake, if we need to talk again before tomorrow's meeting."

Walking away from the Questura, I knew I'd made an impression on Manieri. And that I was certain I was not going to take his advice.

Chapter 33

Sergio was waiting for me when I arrived back at the hotel.

"Miles is here," he said. "He has just flown in, very worried about what you said in the phone call."

I shuddered. I hadn't thought enough about the hurt I must be causing my brother.

"Can I see him?"

"He is sleeping off the jetlag. He asked not to be disturbed."

"You mean he's staying here, in the hotel?"

"He has a room on the floor above yours."

I waited nervously. I tried to take an early lunch but couldn't develop any appetite. I could not stop thinking about where Julia might be. If she'd been kidnapped, what conditions might she be being held in? How frightened had they made her? How well was she bearing up to the ordeal?

And there were gloomier thoughts that would not go away. Just because it had been the woman I now knew was Emelia Rossellini who had died in my arms in the London apartment, it didn't mean that Julia had not also been killed. I knew now I should have been asking Manieri if any bodies had been discovered in the Florence area in the past few days. No doubt Manieri would have been checking on this and, I supposed, it was a measure of the man's respect for my feelings that he had not mentioned it.

It must have been my optimism, the immediate but perhaps in the end ill-fated assumption that Julia was alive, that had closed my mind to this. I tried to shake off my gloomy thoughts but they would not depart. Where was Sergio? I had to wake Miles.

I located Sergio and we took the lift to Miles' room. When we woke him, he was complaining and groggy.

Miles rubbed his eyes. "I asked for three hours. Just three hours, goddammit. I'd barely arrived in Boston when I had to come over here."

"Your brother would not wait," Sergio said.

We'd ordered coffee from room service and when it arrived I requested that it be set down outside the door. Sergio brought it in.

Miles drank a first cupful. "Not hot enough, but strong on caffeine."

"I guess Sergio has told you about the phone call with Hendricks at the Questura," I said.

Miles nodded.

"Miles, I was wrong about Julia. I want you to know that. She may still be alive. I want you and Sergio to help me find her."

"Wait on!" Miles said. "Last night on the phone, you were calling me a murderer."

"OK, I apologise. But don't think that means you didn't behave unbelievably badly. Another woman died. Your investigation of the Landos may have been a factor. Julia has not been found. She's been missing for days; you may also be the cause. Why couldn't you have levelled with me in London?"

"I can't say I don't feel bad about it, Jim. I can't say Sergio and me weren't carried away with the need to minimise the chances of information leaking back to the Landos nor the fact that we were close to breaking our investigation on them wasn't important. No, the regret I have is that I couldn't see past the argument that the more I involved you, the more dangerous it would become for you."

"It already was dangerous," I said. "Being tailed around London."

"I didn't think they would be able to connect you to me. I was being very careful."

"Giving Julia to the Landos. It was unforgivable."

"I couldn't see the harm in it at the time. They really do have the kind of paintings Julia was looking for."

"So you could then pump her for information on the Landos' set up. Hardly the most altruistic thing you've ever done."

"It was part of the thinking, I have to admit." Miles paused and showed genuine contrition. "Look, Jim I'm sorry. I really am. I would do anything I could to go back and undo it. I didn't mean to put you through this. But to be analytical about it, you don't know our investigation was the cause of all this. The police in Florence are investigating the Landos, too."

"Inspector Manieri," I said. "I more or less forced him to admit they were involved. He warned me against prying any further."

"Sergio showed me the photograph of the two women that you sent him. The other woman, the one who died in London, she was the one beside Julia in the photograph?"

"Emelia Rossellini," I said. "Manieri was able to recognise her as the addict and high-class prostitute they'd picked up numerous times. And guess what; the pimp she works for is Matteo Lando."

Miles was unable to hide the seriousness of what he had just heard. His voice lowered. "Then we are all in greater danger than even I'd supposed. We're not safe here in the hotel. We need to move out, now." He turned to look at Sergio. "The safe house in Monteverdi; it's still operational?"

"It's where I am staying now," Sergio said. "I am fairly sure the locals suspect nothing. They think I'm the manager of a tourist souvenir shop here in the city. I do not think they would be too surprised if I had two guests for the next few days."

"Jim, go back to your room and collect your things," Miles said. "Get out as quickly and as surreptitiously as possible. We'll be leaving as soon as we can."

I was surprised at Miles' sudden reaction. Sergio would have told Miles about the abduction in Borgo Pinti. The connection between this and the identity of the murdered woman – the fact that both pointed to Matteo Lando and, more importantly, his father Alfieri – must have been enough to convince Miles we were in danger here. But at last, I thought, they'd begun to take my situation seriously.

Chapter 34

I threw the few things I'd brought with me in the hold all and made sure I had a safe place in it for the laptop and Julia's pocket drive. I took the stairs rather than the lift and within five minutes of the conversation with Miles and Sergio I was ready to approach the reception area to check out.

It was an instinctive reflex I could not explain that made me pause as I rounded the last flight of stairs on the long hotel staircase and prepared to enter the corridor leading to reception. There, walking briskly towards the lift, were two of the men who had abducted me in Borgo Pinti. There was an unmistakable bulge in the waistband of the larger of the two men that showed he still had the gun with him. I drew back, concealing myself behind the corridor corner wall as I watched them scuttle past.

"Room 216," the large man said.

That was my room number.

"And the brother is in 319. Take 216 first." They waited for the lift.

I knew I had to warn Miles. I turned and ran back up the staircase, gambling on the possibility I could climb three flights of stairs carrying the hold-all before the men had found my room, decided it was empty and then proceeded to the third floor.

Taken at speed, it was a punishing climb. I ran out onto the third floor corridor, making my way to Miles' room with the lack of air in my lungs causing real pain.

I banged on the door. There was an interminable wait. Had our attackers already left the second floor? There was sound and movement inside. The door opened, slowly.

"Miles," I said. "They're here. Coming for us."

"Who?"

"Lando's men. Two of the men who abducted me… we've got to get out. Now!"

"I'll get my bags," Miles said.

"No time. Run!"

He grabbed his laptop. "My life, right now," he shouted. "They can have the rest."

I took my brother by the arm and dragged him into the corridor, pushing him towards the staircase. "Run!"

We could hear the lift arriving at the third floor as we ran down the corridor. To get to the staircase, we would have to run past the lift. If the lift doors opened as we went past, the Lando men would see us. But there was no choice. We ran.

I could hear the lift come fully to a stop as it engaged at its third floor location. We'd made it to the top of the staircase. It was a question of whether we would both get far enough down the stairs to be out of the eye line of our attackers as the lift doors opened.

We thought we just might have made it, but there was no way to tell, no chance to look back as we hurtled on down the stairs. There was no gunfire, no sound of the Lando men coming after us. They must have not seen us and must have carried on to Miles' room. "Where is Sergio?" I asked as we reached the second floor.

"He's in the basement car park, picking up his vehicle."

Miles pressed the button to call the lift. I yelled at him in a whisper, "You left your door open and it will take them no time at all to see you're not there. They could be in the lift!"

We ran as quickly as we could down the three flights of stairs to the reception level and then down the additional flights of stairs to the basement car park. As we emerged through the doorway leading on to the lines of parked cars, Sergio drew up.

I shouted, "What the hell is that?"

Sergio was driving an old pickup truck, modified at the rear to take a heavy tow bar. "He uses it to tow a horse box," Miles said. "In his spare time, it's just about all he does, tend to his horses."

We clambered aboard. I was sitting practically on the gear stick as all three of us crammed onto the single seat in the cab.

The lift doors opened to reveal the Lando men. In this subterranean place they must have reasoned that the chances of being observed were small and they both drew their weapons.

As Sergio sped away, tyres squealing on the underground car park concrete, two shots rang out in quick succession. They missed the pickup truck but shattered the windscreens of two cars parked nearby.

A BMW with tinted windows drew up and the Lando men climbed inside but by that time Sergio had climbed the ramp leading to the next level and we were out of range, at least for a moment. He manoeuvred his way to the exit, inserted the token he'd picked up on arrival and passed through the exit barrier.

"They'll soon outrun us in this crate," I said. Sergio set off into the dense traffic surrounding the railway station.

"I am hoping to lose them," Sergio said. He pulled off into a side street and then took a sharp left followed by a sharp right turn. However, when I looked behind, there was the BMW, gaining on us.

It didn't seem as if Lando's men were going to risk gunning us down out here in broad daylight, rather, they'd settled for the idea of following closely and waiting for an opportunity to ambush us in a more secluded place. They settled in behind the pickup truck and, wherever it went, they would follow, biding their time.

"So what do we do now?" I asked. We'd made it to the A11 Autostrada and taken our place in the centre lane, heading towards Viareggio. "They're just waiting to pick us off."

"There is a way," said Sergio. "But it does involve some risk."

"What kind of risk?" Miles asked.

"Maybe it is better not to think too much about it. Just make sure your seatbelts are fastened but don't let them see you doing it. Make it look as if you are sitting just normally."

Sergio raised his speed from 50 to 70 miles per hour, doing this gradually over a distance of about a mile. The BMW responded, increasing speed but keeping the same two car lengths distance behind.

"When I sound the horn, brace yourself."

Before there was time to think about this, Sergio sounded the horn. At the same time, he applied the brakes as sharply as he could, decelerating the pickup truck with a loud squeal of the tyres. There was a sudden and deafening thud behind us as the BMW crashed into the back of the pickup truck. We were thrown forward by the impact but the seat belts held.

"No airbags?" Miles shouted.

"Too old," Sergio shouted back. He was struggling to keep control of the still-moving truck. It had been momentarily shunted out of its lane. He regained control and looked in the rear view mirror.

"That should do it." He smiled as he caught sight of the BMW, its whole front folded in on itself like a concertina, air bags deployed. As he watched, a vehicle following behind the BMW smashed into its rear, shunting it off the road.

"So much damage," I said. "And the pickup truck is just about untouched."

"It's the tow bar," Sergio said. "Colliding with that at 70 miles per hour would create the kind of damage you get with a wrecking ball on a building. And the fact that the BMW is one of the best-designed cars in the world. Those crumple zones really do crumple."

We left the highway at the next exit, returning to the road and travelling back in the direction we'd come from. Within a few minutes we were witnessing the conse-quences of our recent actions, now taking place on the opposite carriageway. Blue lights flashed as the rescue services were arriving at the accident scene. A stranded BMW, folded up at the front and rear stood stranded at the side of the road. The estate car that had collided with it from the rear had also pulled up.

The collapse of the BMW had clearly saved the occu-pants. As we passed by in the pickup truck, the Lando men were being cut from the wreckage, shaken, dazed but protected from the suddenness of the reduction in momentum that had been inflicted upon them. I was almost sure that the large Lando man saw us as we passed on the opposite carriageway and gave a cold stare.

The remainder of the trip to Monteverdi was uneventful. Within half an hour the pickup truck was safely stowed away in the garage that backed onto Sergio's house.

"I don't think we'll be using that again for a while," Sergio said. "I know a place with very good rates on a hire car with a tow bar."

I was pleased we'd shown the Landos we could fight back.

Part Four

Florence, six days earlier
Thursday August 28th to Saturday August 30th

Chapter 35

Thursday August 28th

Giuseppe arrived at the hotel as expected and drove Julia once more to the Lando estate outside of Lucca. Julia was busy making the scans of the paintings selected for the day when Alessa Lando appeared at the study door. Giuseppe, who had been watching Julia as diligently as ever came to attention.

"Have you started again?" Something in Alessa's intonation made the question sound more than a factual enquiry.

"Yes, it's going fine," Julia said. She sensed the tension Alessa had introduced into what should have been a more grateful appreciation that the work was going well.

"Well, I suggest you pack up and leave right away," Alessa said. "We Landos, we're not used to being made fools of – how do you say – being taken for a ride?"

"I have no idea what you are so concerned about," Julia said. She was trying to make her voice stay calm. There was threat, real threat in Alessa's words and in her hostile manner.

Alessa was holding the agreement they'd signed apportioning any monies to be gained if Julia discovered anything beneath the Lando's paintings. She held up the paperwork and ripped it into pieces smaller than confetti and threw the fragments up into the air. "This is what I think of your agreement!"

"I have a copy of the agreement we both signed," Julia said.

"Not worth anything." Alessa smiled. "The agreement is under Italian jurisdiction; no Italian court is going to even hear any claim you may think you can make."

Julia could see that Giuseppe was preparing to grab hold of her and she was suddenly starting to feel very afraid, as if she'd known that the menace he'd been barely concealing all along would have to emerge sooner rather than later.

"Tell me what's wrong," Julia said. "What's changed?"

"Let's say the doubts I had from the start that you were not all you seemed have been confirmed," Alessa said. "You were very foolish to think I would be taken in."

"Taken in by what?"

"Don't think there is any mileage in playing the innocent, I know what you are really doing here."

"I'm scanning your paintings, looking for underpaintings, helping you discover a hidden masterpiece. That's it. That's all I'm doing here. There is no other agenda."

"You have one chance to tell the truth, to let me know why you are really here."

"I'm telling the truth. I'm here to help you."

"So why do I have it on very good authority that you're here to pry into the affairs of the Lando family?" Alessa recalled her real shock when Albertini in the Ministry had confirmed all Zella had told her. "You should know we have influence. There is no one here who would pay any attention to any evidence you might have obtained."

"I won't be intimidated if that's what you mean," Julia said. "If you won't listen to reason, when I tell you there is no 'evidence', no ulterior motive, just the scans, that's all."

"I want all the data you have collected in my possession by 5.30 tomorrow," Alessa said. "Giuseppe will make sure you comply. Tell anyone about this and I promise you will not live to regret it. Nor will they. If you've sent any of the data to anyone we will find them and track it down. Do you understand?"

Giuseppe had hold of Julia's arm and was forcing it up her back, delivering a sudden shock of pain that left no doubt Alessa was serious in her disrespect for the law.

Julia began to cry. "You've got to believe me. I'm doing just what I say I'm doing. I am exactly who I say I am. There is nothing else to tell."

"I don't believe the material you have been collecting has anything to do with searching for missing master-pieces. You're just here to gather evidence on what pictures we own, to build an inventory. So for what? To look for stolen pictures? To make a case that we owe taxes? What you were sent here to obtain. So I want it all back. Whatever you have running on the university computers; whatever you have on the PC you have here in the study. Anything you might have on your laptop. And just pray to God you haven't compromised anyone else by sending them anything. We will find them. We will hunt them down."

Julia was not just feeling frightened. She was feeling foolish for not having taken Anna's advice about steering clear of the Landos.

Giuseppe released her. He stepped back with a sadistic smile.

"We are going to be taking you back to your hotel in Florence," Alessa said. "Don't do anything foolish. Do not tell anyone what is happening. Go to the university and recover the data. Tell no one. Give us back all you have taken and tell no one and we just might come to an arrangement that allows you to leave this country safely."

Julia could not hide her shock at the sudden barbarity of Alessa's threats.

"Now, why don't you want to tell us why you are really here?"

"There's nothing I can tell you."

"Have it your way. We'll get the data back first. Then we'll set about finding out why you're really here." Alessa turned her back and walked from the room, leaving Julia to Giuseppe.

There was silence as the scanning equipment was packed away. A number of the paintings had not been investigated. It didn't seem to matter now.

The drive back along the A11 Autostrada to Florence was similarly silent, save for the tinny Europop on the car radio.

Julia couldn't concentrate on the views of the Tuscan countryside. She could only think of how things had changed so suddenly and the fact that the Landos were now an outright threat.

Back in the hotel room alone she fought back her tears.

She felt foolish that she could have thought women like Alessa Lando could be trusted.

No matter how many times she thought her situation through, she returned to the same point: make it look like she was following their wishes. It was all she could do. She was concerned they might make a connection to Jim, or to Emelia.

What they didn't know was that the information from the scans she'd taken so far would have been processed by the time she arrived at the university the next morning to collect the data, as Alessa Lando had insisted on calling it. She had seemingly lost all interest in what might lie beneath those paintings she so ostentatiously displayed on the walls of her house. Despite everything, that was an interest Julia still could not bury.

Chapter 36

Clinton Ridley felt at home in Florence. It was a place meant for him. It seemed at times that the culture, the art, the history of aesthetic achievement had all along been waiting for a man of his quality to receive it and enjoy it. It was somehow part of the natural order of things that he should have come of age here as a young man, discovering himself, his essence, in the beauty all around him.

He was thinking these things as he walked across the Ponte Vecchio, working his way towards the Oltrarno district where the more bohemian element lived and worked – away from the clutter of the tourist traps that the Duomo and Santa Maria Novella districts had become.

And he thought also of the other coming-of-age that Florence had presented him. The women of Oltrarno, he wouldn't call them prostitutes, who had given him his first taste of love. Some would call it lust, perhaps, but he knew the difference. What did it matter that you had to pay? The girls around the Termini needed to make a living, after all. Yes, this had been the beginning of the awareness of love in his life and it was this that he would return to each time he visited the beautiful city.

But not today. Not yet, anyway.

He was meeting Zella DeFrancesco. She had been difficult to track down. It had taken more than one bribe.

She was in a position to let him know what Julia was doing here, searching for her masterpiece. And along the way he would let this stalwart of the Lando family know just what he thought about Julia's activities with their paintings here.

They were seated at one of the tables outside a small restaurant in Piazza San Spirito. "She's out of control as far as the Clinton Ridley Studios is concerned," he said after the formalities had been completed. "I've tried to make her respond to the expectations of an internationally recognised studio but she refuses."

Zella shifted in her seat. She didn't like the man but he might prove to be useful. "You haven't come here to waste my time in office controversies, have you Dr Ridley?"

"Clinton, it's Clinton – no it's more than that. I know for a fact that Julia Blake has no intention of telling the Lando family anything if she finds a painting of real value."

"And how do you know this, Clinton?"

"It's what I have reluctantly had to deduce after all the attempts to get her to open up to me, her employer, about what she is really doing out here. She's obsessed. It's more than a job to her, it's a reputation, it's a future. Somehow the search for a masterpiece has consumed her."

"Those are forceful words."

"Yes, but there is no other way to explain it. If she finds anything she will not reveal it. I'm sure of it."

"I think you may be right. And I believe she may already have found something."

Ridley leaned forward. "What have you heard?"

"Reports from the house in Lucca where she is scanning the Lando paintings. I have it on good authority that Signora Blake became very excited after scanning one of the paintings. Yet she chose to say nothing."

"It's as I told you."

"She became very furtive, she tried to make it seem as if nothing had happened, but the people there saw the look in her eyes, perhaps a look of discovery."

Ridley's pulse raced. "Any indication of what she'd found?"

"It's not at all clear. Giuseppe, who had been told to stay with her at all times, told me she mentioned something about a swan."

"*Leda and the Swan*. I knew it. I knew she was close. We could do a deal, you and I. If you could obtain the painting, the one that Julia became excited about, somehow spirit it away from the Landos, I could restore it. I could remove the overpainting and put it on the market. It wouldn't have to go to an open auction. There are collectors who would buy such a painting without any questions being asked."

"Let me think about it, Clinton. It would not be easy."

"Half of fifty million might make it worthwhile." He smiled. He thrust out his hand.

Zella shook it. The Englishman in the pretentious clothes was hooked. It was remarkable how easily he'd accepted the lie about the painting. "We have a deal."

"Let me know when you are able to get hold of the painting."

"It may take some time. I'll let you know when I have something."

Ridley said farewell and headed off to celebrate with the girls of Oltrarno.

Chapter 37

Alfieri Lando sat in the only chair in his inner sanctum. He was wearing the cape and had laid down the mask. He had taken up a favourite cigar that he now smoked with satisfaction.

In here, in the secret room, was his greatest secret. He looked with pride at the Michelangelo hanging on the wall opposite. How foolish people like the English woman were to try to find a treasure as a mere underpainting when all along here it was on display only for him in all its glory.

It had long been in the Lando family, the source of their continuing power. It was over three hundred years since they'd tricked the King of France out of the Michelangelo, smuggling it back to Italy where it belonged. And since then it had remained in Lando hands, fulfilling its destiny as a symbol, no, more than a symbol, the reality, of their dominance. It had survived Napoleon, survived the fascists. The Landos had proven their ability to protect it over twelve generations.

He'd raised Matteo just as he himself had been raised; with none of the emotion or moral scruples that befuddled the ordinary people of this town. Raised with the potential to be special; as special as he himself had become. Matteo had been prepared for a great destiny just as his own father had prepared him.

And here it was – *Leda and the Swan*. It spoke to him, told him how special he was.

If he looked long enough the figures would come to life. The god was half-man, half-bird – this of course was the appearance he'd chosen at that moment. And Leda, his choice, the one he'd decided to impregnate beyond all the other mortals he could have chosen.

And the ghost woman, the worrying extra figure, the female figure of his nightmares, the portent of danger yet to come; the reason to be secretive, to be cautious, to make sure even Matteo should not be let into the secret, at least until the time came.

Could a man become a god? It was a feeble question. As he sat in the chair, smoking the cigar, looking at the painting, he was a god. It could not be doubted. How else had the Lando family prevailed against all the odds, against their foes over all these years? And how else could he be absolutely sure their power would endure for another three hundred years?

Just as he'd learned to savour the power he had acquired to choose who to take for his pleasure – just as he'd taken Emelia Rossellini – so he'd learned to savour the power of life and death he exercised over the mortals that surrounded him. Just as he'd removed most of the Rossellinis, to leave just the bare husk of a family.

There were those that, if they knew of its existence, would value the Michelangelo in monetary terms; what was it the English woman expected – fifty million at auction? How these Philistines had missed the point. His *Leda* was worth ten times that; the source of his power, the driving force of an empire that made fifty million every single year.

How essential that he kept all this secret from Alessa, just as his father had kept the painting a secret from his own mother. Alessa was a thorn in his side, the necessary corrective keeping him sane, the spying partner who tested his guile in exercising his power so it didn't become all-consuming. Yes, it was essential for her not to know, for her to seek to limit him without knowing the extent of what he was entitled to do. For, if she knew, she would certainly have realised how futile that was.

He was pleased that everyone, including Alessa, was so sure he had no interest in art. This was true. He was interested only in this one painting, all others paled in comparison.

Alfieri flipped open the laptop and inserted the DVD. He enjoyed reliving his conquests. There was Emelia, lying on the chair, waiting for him. And here he came in wearing cape and mask, a true god at the peak of his power, taking her as he wished.

Yes, he would see Emelia again. Zella had arranged it.

But what was this? The slip of the mask. Emelia looking at him. Had she seen? Did she know it was him? That was a problem he would have to solve as quickly as he could.

Chapter 38

Despite what had happened at Lucca and the sudden withdrawal of access to the paintings by Alessa Lando, Julia still couldn't keep down a feeling of elation. It was because she'd found Emelia.

There was a sense of completeness now that had answered those feelings she'd been having all these years that something was missing in her life.

Missing despite her love for Jim.

Missing despite the success she'd achieved in her career as a conservator.

Now Emelia was here, was known to her, the missing piece had been found and nothing should be allowed to change that.

The world was so different now. Its hard edge had been softened, made lighter, more illuminated. It was as if her world had been a painting obscured by darkened varnish that had now been removed. Only she was not looking in any more at someone else's life, she was looking out into a brightened world and the new clarity all around her.

She was trying to piece together the chain of events in Emelia's life. She felt guilty that her own life was so privileged while Emelia's was so hard.

What mattered now was that she should help Emelia. To help her escape. She knew little about this squalid world but she knew enough to realise they would not let Emelia go easily.

They'd agreed to meet in the Piazza di San Firenze and walk among the crowds out shopping or heading towards the Uffizi. Emelia said she felt safer there, with less chance of being followed by one of the Lando informers who would report back what she was doing.

Julia could hardly recognise her. She was dressed in brown trousers, a steel grey duffle coat and her hair was tucked up into a corduroy cap. She looked quite masculine. As they met, Julia linked arms with her; to the casual observer they were like any other loving couple setting out to see the sights.

"I have to tell you something," Emelia said. "It is something you may find hard to understand, knowing as I do the different lives we have been living."

Julia said nothing. She was aware that almost anything she might say would seem to be the easy words of someone who just didn't know the harshness of the life her sister had been forced to endure.

"I thought long and hard about whether I should tell you this," Emelia said. "I don't want you to feel any worse about having a person like me as your sister, but I have to tell someone and you are one of the few people in this whole town who I feel I can trust, so I have to take the risk of losing you."

"Don't think that way, Emelia. There's nothing you can say that would make me want to lose you. I've only just found you."

"How can I be sure?"

"Tell me. I'll understand."

As they walked amongst the crowds taking them along the narrow Via de' Gondi and out onto Piazza della Signora, Emelia told Julia about the rape, about how she discovered it was Alfieri Lando behind the mask. How she couldn't let them know she'd discovered it was him. She told Julia about her love for Matteo. How good it had been. How she'd still loved him even when he'd turned her out as a rich man's whore. She was fighting to hold back the tears. "What I'll never be able to come to terms with is his part in the rape. He didn't care about what happened to me."

"You still love him?"

"No. The love died. It died when I knew he would not protect me from his father."

"Did he know?"

"It doesn't matter. He didn't care when I told him."

"I'm sorry you've lost him."

What must it be like to be driven so low, to be enmeshed in the world the Landos policed? What hypocrisy, the way Alessa Lando postured at the love of art with a painting collection in the house at Lucca. It was nothing more than a temple to the deception they had fostered – that they were an Italian family of quality when all along they were riven with corruption and they used their position to rule by fear. Anna had been right to warn her against them.

"Do you have someone?" Emelia asked.

"Jim. James is his proper name. I can't imagine what would happen that would come between us." As soon as she said this she realised that her happiness, just as her privileged background, could easily become a barrier between her and her sister.

"Just as I thought about Matteo."

"But at least you know it is over; maybe there is some comfort in that."

"There will never be any comfort for a woman like me. It's going to happen again."

"What's going to happen?"

"Another meeting with Alfieri. He's asked Zella to arrange it again. I don't think I can take it."

"Matteo still does nothing to stop this?"

"He does nothing."

"Then you have to leave."

"I can't leave. You don't understand. I am owned. A piece of property. You don't know how deadly they would be to protect that."

"You just walk away."

"Walk away where? They have people everywhere. At the airports, at the railway stations; they give them a few hundred to keep them informed about anything and everything. It's nothing to them. The information they pay for is useless most of the time. But nothing passes them by in this town. I wouldn't get more than a few miles."

"There has to be a way." Julia gripped her sister's arm more tightly. "You shouldn't have worried about telling me. There's nothing that could change what we have between us."

They mingled with the crowds outside the Uffizi, enjoying the street performers and, for the moment, felt safe in being anonymous there.

Chapter 39

The sun beat down from a too-blue sky. As Giancarlo Orletti walked up the steep steps to the asphalt apron that led onto the church at San Berado, he was already beginning to sweat. But this was no time to be concerned about such things. He'd at last got some information on the Lando activity with Emelia's help.

He sat on the stone wall that formed the perimeter of the church grounds, poised high on the hill overlooking the city. From up here you could see the old town sat low and trembling beneath the mighty presence of the Duomo, the red tiled roofs pressed down by the weight of all that redeemable sin. The sun shone its unforgiving, unhelpful light on the tragic terrain. Unnoticeable from this distance, in the warren-like streets intersecting the pressed down buildings, mere humans walked, clinging to the shade of those narrow streets, hoping not to be seen by their vengeful God.

Sergio Romani arrived, a few minutes later than expected, and sat beside Giancarlo without a word of greeting.

Just in their eye line, an old priest, dressed in the black cassock of his Order, emerged from a side door of the church and began his diagonal walk across the asphalt apron towards the small office in the corner of the grounds. Both men watched. Giancarlo could see from the priest's gait and his mannerisms that this was a walk he made many times each day. Something he had manufactured as a personal addition to the ritual that dominated his life in the Olivetan Order. Something designed to break the monotony of the silent chamber from which he'd emerged, perhaps in the hope of meeting and exchanging a nod or a word with someone, anyone, or perhaps just for the pleasure of being seen in the cassock and reminding those watching that he was a man of piety and standing. Something of the predictability of his walk told him about the patterns of life that kept people trapped in their lives.

When the priest disappeared from view into the office, Giancarlo spoke. "We are both Florentines who want to make this town a better place."

"If only it was that simple."

"People like us, we can make a difference."

"I don't have such lofty ambitions. I'm just looking for a story, one to sell more newspapers. I don't have any other agenda."

Giancarlo looked again at the scene spread out before him. He thought of Emelia. He knew the risks she must have taken to get information like this – that this man, Sergio Romani, was investigating the Lando operation.

"We have enough in common, at least enough to want to help each other." Giancarlo paused. "I know you have been investigating the Landos. Give me something I can use."

Sergio was aware of the risks of revealing anything. The man could be informing for the Landos. But if he only revealed what they already knew, he would be giving nothing away and it was just possible the policeman might be straight. "We've heard the Landos are planning a major move later this week. A large consignment. Lethal. Six thousand metric tonnes of liquid PCBs. Polychlorinated biphenyls. You know, the stuff they used to cool electrical plant before they found out it was a major carcinogen. Dump it in the sea and it enters the food chain. They've found it in Inuit mother's milk in northern Canada, one of the remotest places on the planet. The mothers ate the seals that ate the fish that ingested the PCBs and concentrated it in their fat. They end up with levels of toxicity up to seventy times higher than normal. The stuff is out there on a world wide scale."

"Where? Where are they moving the stuff from?"

"The industrial suburbs of Milan. There is a large generating plant there being decommissioned. Rich pickings for the company that charges a premium rate to dispose of the waste in an environmentally responsible way."

Giancarlo nodded. "There will be the pretence at least of disposing of it legally. There is a lot of paper work involved; people holding PCB containing equipment have to register it. The Interior Ministry will be monitoring what they do. But the Landos have the means to find a way round that. So when? When are they moving it?"

"We don't know exactly. Sometime later this week. That's all we can be certain of."

"Your source?"

"You know I can't tell you."

"Tell me when you hear more. That's not a request. I'll build up the case with Inspector Manieri, get him to authorise the manpower."

The old priest reappeared from the office and began to recross the courtyard, disappearing back into the church. Though nothing was said, both men knew it would be a long time before much changed in their country.

"Come on," Giancarlo said. "I want to show you something."

They walked across the courtyard towards the corner area that the priest had covered in his stately walk, then turned down a narrow alleyway past a shop selling flowers for the mourners and made their way to the large graveyard at the rear of the church.

"This is where Florence's finest come to be buried," Giancarlo said.

They walked through the sprawling graveyard. Every available space had been taken by graves with ever more elaborate and imposing headstones, many taking the form of larger than life sculptures. Built into the walls surrounding the graveyard were tombs tiered on four or five levels like high-rise apartments. The effect of so many crammed together artefacts posturing at importance was to render them all insignificant, an elaborate expression of hubris.

And here on this burning blue sky summer day, the acrid smell of decay.

"If you want to stand out from the crowd," Giancarlo said, "you have to have a mausoleum."

The Lando mausoleum. It was an imposing, dark stone structure with a wrought iron door. The door was open. A workman was inside, decorating. Inside there was a chapel.

Giancarlo smiled. "In life as in death, you have to keep up appearances. There are more than ten generations of

Landos rotting in there. That's how long they've held sway in this town."

"With the blessing of the Church."

"As long as they finally repent and make the right contribution, why would it be a problem?"

Sergio understood what Orletti was saying by bringing him here. They would need all their courage to take on a corrupting power that had held power in this town for all these years.

Chapter 40

Matteo Lando watched the two men from a distance. Who did they think they were, staring at the Lando mausoleum, talking about the family, no doubt?

He'd been following the policeman on and off since he had been seen meeting Emelia close to the Academia. But who was the man with him? He looked familiar, but he couldn't recall where he'd seen him. Perhaps somewhere in town? He thought he would recognise him if he saw him again. He wished he'd brought the long lens camera, pretending to be a tourist; he could have photographed him and had him identified. Now he had a problem. The two men were about to separate and he was here alone. There would not be time to call any of his men. He might have to do this on his own.

Matteo decided to stick with the policeman. He'd discovered that his name was Orletti. It was a question of assessing which risk was the greater. Instinct told him the two men had been engaged in planning and the one most able to implement any kind of action would be with the police. So, he had to let the unknown man go, watch him walk away with a wave. But Orletti stayed there, by the mausoleum, biding his time, making sure he would not be seen leaving with his accomplice. A fatal mistake.

Killing a policeman, that would cause a hue and cry. The police would always protect their own, step up their activities to track down the killer. But if the body was never found, there would be no alert, no additional police activities to worry about. So that decided it, there and then, there was no need to think about it anymore.

Giancarlo was disabled before he had time to respond. An arm of immense strength was clamped round his chest, pinning his arms.

The muzzle of a gun was pressed into the base of his neck. He was frog-marched to the small white decorator's van parked on the pathway, pushed inside and made to lie face down on the floor of the van.

The decorator, Trentoni, calmly stopped painting. He gave Matteo a knowing look and said, "Signor Lando, tell me what you want me to do."

They bound Giancarlo's feet with electrical cabling used in the restoration and they did the same with his hands, binding them behind his back. Trentoni drove the van while Matteo crouched beside Giancarlo, the gun still held to the police officer's head. They arrived at a disused building near the railway at Rifredi, drove in, closed the doors and cut the van engine.

Matteo turned Giancarlo over so he could see his face. "No point shouting. No one will hear you."

"I'm a policeman. You know if anything happens to me you'll have every officer in Florence looking for you."

"Not if no one finds you. I want answers. I want to know what you've been doing prying into the affairs of my family. I want to know what you've been planning with Emelia Rossellini. I want to know who you've just met and what plans you were making with him."

Matteo withdrew the nine-inch stiletto he carried in a tailored pocket inside his jacket and held it over Giancarlo's heart.

"You're going to kill me anyway, so why should I say a word?"

"A brave man, that's a remarkable thing. Not so brave now."

Matteo inserted the stiletto into the flesh above Giancarlo's ribs just to the right side of his heart. There was searing pain. He struggled, but the bonds held him tight so he couldn't move. Blood began to flow; he could feel the shirt under his jacket becoming warm and sticky.

"The next one is in the heart. And then you will die. Tell me. Tell me what I want to know."

"Go to hell, where you belong."

Matteo frowned. It had gone wrong. The stiletto had entered the heart. The policeman was starting to convulse, blood forming in his eyes.

Matteo closed the van doors and walked round to the front of the vehicle where the decorator was waiting. "Nothing more to do here, Trentoni. Back to San Berado. Make it seem that nothing out of place has happened. Say nothing. The future of your children depends on it."

Giancarlo was alone on the cold van floor, bleeding. He knew he was going to die. He thought of Emelia and how he should have done more to tell her about his real feelings for her.

Chapter 41

It had taken careful planning. It began with Julia leaving the Hotel Leonardo with her luggage. When she checked out the hotel manager was not there but she had been signed out by his assistant – 9:30 AM, Friday, August 29th. It was now a matter of record. But whoever might be tipping off the Landos would take some time to know she was gone.

Julia picked up the taxi that the hotel had summoned and asked the driver to take her to the airport at Bergamo. The driver checked that she could afford the 200 km journey that would take them north beyond Milan, but she told him the flight was cheap so his charge was not an issue. He seemed pleased to have chanced upon such a lucrative commission.

Not long after they'd set out she leaned forward. "I'm sorry, I should have told you, I have a friend who is going to see me off at the airport."

The driver looked at her through the rear view mirror. "You should have said. Where are they?"

"Outside the gardens on Viale Giacomo Matteoti." It was a small deception, but one that Julia hoped would allow Emelia to slip away without notice.

As arranged, Emelia was waiting.

Emelia had made her way to the gardens without difficulty. She'd dropped the masculine attire and now wore heavy makeup and the regulation mini, boob tube and knee-high boots of her profession. As he drew up and stopped, the taxi driver looked her over in the Italian way that showed desire but caused no offence. She smiled and then climbed in and joined her sister on the back seat.

"Right on time," Emelia said.

"As we arranged," Julia replied.

They'd decided to say only what was required. They wanted the driver to have a clear idea of the two women and their appearance so if, like so many, he was to report to the Landos, he would present a clear picture in the way they wanted.

"I hope you will enjoy being in London once again," Emelia said. She was following their pre-prepared script.

"It will be the first time in five weeks. My husband will not remember me. And you?"

"I have my man. I will be happy with him."

They were aware that the driver was listening intently, but as their small talk went on he became progressively less interested and, no more than fifteen minutes into the journey, he turned up the volume on the in-car radio and began listening to the inane Italian pop that married last year's US chart music with the emotionalism that seemed to be essential in this country. With that, the two women could relax and watch the Tuscan scenery pass by, making idle conversation, counting every one of the three hours as they put distance between them and the horrors awaiting Emelia in Florence.

The citizens of Bergamo were relatively new to the cheap flight economy. The small airport that had been underused was now filled with tourists who all, on arrival, were seeking to be somewhere else. Either north to the Italian Lakes or south to Florence and Milan. The trick was to relieve as many of them as possible of their cash before they moved on and hence benefit the struggling local economy. It was the near anarchy this entailed that had attracted Julia. The Lando influence, she thought, would be much less prominent here.

As they drew to a halt at the airport, Julia paid the driver. She gave him a tip that he would remember. Emelia made sure the driver took in her appearance once more by coming up close to him and thanking him personally.

"You want me to stay?" he asked. "To take you back to Firenze?"

"No," Emelia said. "It's over an hour before take off. I'll get another taxi home."

They took the luggage and headed for the small public-side cafe.

"Do you think anyone has followed us?" Emelia asked.

Julia shook her head. "I'll get the coffee."

There was a small risk in the plan. They would both go to the washroom at the same time, leaving the bags. A zealous airport official could report the bags as suspicious objects and take them away for inspection. That would mean they would be subject to questioning when Julia was identified as the owner. But since Bergamo was a small provincial airport, the betting was the bags would not arouse suspicion. It was a risk they had to take.

The ladies' washroom was primitive but functional for their needs. They occupied two of the cubicles, side by side. Julia carefully removed her clothes and handed them over the cubicle dividing wall to Emelia who handed her own clothes back.

Julia tried to think herself into the mindset of her sister, like an actress trying to think her way into a new role. It was about manner as much as appearance and she'd been privileged to only a few days to observe her sister. The mini showed too much of her legs for comfort and the boob tube really did emphasise her boobs. She shuffled out of the cubicle, unsteady on the high-heeled boots. Emelia emerged a moment later. The two women looked at each other and laughed.

"You don't look a lot like me," Emelia said. "I have to work on your makeup."

"But more to the point," Julia said, "you could easily be taken for me in those clothes once we take off most of your makeup."

They had to act quickly. Julia worked with the cosmetics from Emelia's makeup bag, adding false eyelashes, plenty of mascara and heavy red lipstick. It wouldn't have passed the test at any beauty salon but her resulting appearance was enough like Emelia to pass. For Emelia, it was a matter of removing the makeup she had on and applying just a few light touches of cosmetic. Julia was surprised at the rapidity of the transformation. It showed, she thought, there was indeed no real difference between them but what circumstance had placed in their way. They had achieved the identity swap without anyone entering.

Back at the cafe, the luggage remained untouched. There was no sign of any security guard involvement; their absence had passed without incident.

Julia handed over her bag. "Take it. Inside you'll find my passport. Use your phone to call me to let me know you have passed security and are about to board. Then leave it on the plane in case they try to track you. There's also a paperback in English. Take it out; look as though you're reading it. It will reinforce the impression that you're English."

"I won't understand a word," Emelia said.

"It won't matter. It's the impression that counts. Now you're me, make every one of the English words you know count. If in doubt, nod and smile. You'd be surprised how far it will take you."

"I can't thank you enough for what you are doing for me. You must promise me you will take great care the rest of the time you are here."

The remainder of the plan was simple. When Emelia reached London, she would go to the apartment overlooking the Thames. Julia would let Jim know she would be arriving. It had made no sense to tell him earlier, he would only have been worried about what Julia was getting herself into. But as a fait accompli, he would understand and keep Emelia safe there. On arrival at the apartment, Emelia would ask Jim to post Julia's passport to her. She'd written on a piece of paper in her bag the address of the hotel she'd planned to stay in for the next few days while the passport arrived. At the Hotel Savoy she'd left a further change of clothes that would return her to her expected role in life as a leading conservator. Then she would work on placating Alessa Lando by returning the data she'd collected on the paintings. If all went well, as she prayed it would, she could then book a flight from Bergamo back to England. Some issues with passport control back home could arise, but she would explain everything, and then finally be reunited with both Jim and Emelia in London.

Time passed slowly as they waited for the departure to be called. They would have to part; they knew they didn't want to face up to this. The time they'd been together was so short and it seemed unthinkable they should now be separated by over one thousand miles. But there was no choice; it had to be done if Emelia was ever to escape from the Landos.

"Go," Julia said at last. "I'll be all right. And I'll be seeing you in London in three or four day's time. We can spend all the time we want together then."

Emelia embraced her and looked deeply into her eyes. "Thank you, dear sister." And with that she turned and walked with the luggage towards the check-in gate.

Julia watched from a short distance as the airline agent checked the passport and asked who had packed the bags. There was not going to be a problem; Emelia was quite accomplished at passing herself off as the English woman pictured in the passport. Within a few minutes the boarding pass was issued and the luggage was tagged and sent down onto the conveyor belt to be transported to the hold. Emelia turned and waved. She headed through the doorway to flight-side and was lost to sight.

A middle-aged man sat next to Julia and began looking her over. It was all too easy to forget what she must now look like, how available to such a man she must seem. She longed to get away from the airport, to get back to the hotel and out of Emelia's clothes. But she would not leave until she knew Emelia was safely away.

Julia took out her own mobile phone and pretended to make a call. She began talking into it as if she was talking to a client, making arrangements to meet him in half an hour's time. The middle-aged man stood up and walked away.

The phone rang. It was Emelia. "I have passed security, there was no problem, they thought I was you. We board the plane now. I will see you in London, dear sister."

"I've forgotten something," Julia said. "Inside the book, there is a message from Giancarlo. He wanted me to give it to you, but I didn't want to delay your leaving. I thought you might stay if you saw it. So I hid it in the book. And you have it now. I think he means what he says in the message. One day soon when we get through all this you should find him."

"I understand. I have to go. I'll see you in London."

Julia was about to leave when another man came to sit beside her. "Emelia," he said, "Signor Lando is very disappointed you are here."

Chapter 42

Julia was walked out of the airport building towards a limousine parked nearby. It was staged to look like an everyday event; a woman being met at the airport by a chauffeur-driven hire car. The bulky man who had accosted her inside the airport building, who told her his name was Lorenzo, was even carrying one of those clipboards used to announce the name of the person being met. But the reality was that Julia was being taken away to some place she didn't know and it was useless to protest.

Try to act like Emelia. This was what she had to do. To keep up the pretence as long as possible so Emelia could be sure of landing in London without being met by a similar welcoming party.

Julia's Italian was passable but she had not yet acquired any of the colloquialism of the language as used by these people. She'd spoken with Emelia for only a few hours and there had been little chance to catch her take on the language. Julia decided to say as little as possible and to act out her new role as convincingly as she could.

The clothes and the makeup helped. These men were used to treating women like her with disdain and to require little but subservience. So the language, pared down to a few apologetic-sounding phrases and comments, might suffice for a while. In the end, she knew, this was the best chance she had of aiding Emelia's escape.

They'd reached the black limousine. Lorenzo held open the rear door. "Get in."

Julia said nothing. She attempted to climb into the back seat in the short, short skirt without showing the modesty she would have displayed herself. Lorenzo caressed her upper thigh with a massive hand. She smiled back. He seemed satisfied with the normality of events. Inside, Julia was fighting to control an anger she couldn't show.

Lorenzo called over his accomplice who was talking with one of the taxi drivers. He sat in the front passenger seat in the limousine with Lorenzo driving. They set off at a sedate pace before picking up speed as they headed towards the E64 Autostrada Milano-Brescia that led to Milan.

They seemed to have little interest in her. Julia could hear them talking about what they were doing in Milan. Something about a shipment going to be made later that week. Something they had to get right or risk being taken to task by the Lando hierarchy. But their language was full of slang and references to people and places she didn't know and they had a criminal way of speaking that the world over was meant to be incomprehensible if over-heard. She couldn't follow the full details. But it didn't matter now. As time passed as they cruised the Autostrada, she was thinking of Emelia and the fact that her safe arrival in London was getting closer with every minute.

She was thinking of how she might contact Jim. They'd not taken her phone away, but it was going to be difficult to use it as, every minute or so, Lorenzo was giving her searching looks through the rear-view mirror. The phone was in her bag; she just had to reach in and take it out without arousing suspicion. The bag had a magnetic clasp that was difficult to open without making a noise. She kept looking out of the window, pretending to be looking at the passing countryside. She'd managed to get the clasp open but she had made a small noise as the bag had sprung open.

Lorenzo's eyes, reflected in the mirror, dwelt on her longer this time. "You're getting uncomfortable?"

"No, I'm OK."

The eyes moved away. She had the phone now and was able to place it face up on the seat beside her. Lorenzo's eyes flickered her way again and then returned once more to the road ahead. She couldn't be sure how much of her could be seen through the rearview mirror but she reasoned that since Lorenzo hadn't seen the phone as it lay on the seat beside her, so long as she kept it there and was careful not to be seen looking at it, it should escape his attention.

She passed her fingertips over the dial buttons of the phone. Without looking at it, she tried to recall the placing of the various keys. She found the *on* button. Did the phone make a noise as soon as it was switched on? Would the screen make enough light to be noticed? She should have been able to remember but in this moment she could not. She took a risk and turned it on.

Lorenzo's eyes were on her again. She kept her gaze on the countryside. The eyes moved away.

Julia had a sudden fear that someone might ring. She had to hope. Perhaps she could allow herself the very shortest look down at the phone. If it was quick enough, and if she could desynchronise this with Lorenzo's attentions, she may be able to get a message out.

The eyes returned. Julia looked at the countryside. If he saw her eyes moving away, he would know she'd been waiting to see when he was looking at her. The anticipation was more an instinct, to look away just before his eyes would appear in the mirror. It was not perfect, but it was working well enough.

Choosing her moment, she glanced down at the phone menu, scrolled and selected *e-mail*. She returned to looking out of the window just before Lorenzo's eyes appeared again in the mirror. Some half-dozen iterations later, she looked down again, scrolled and selected *new message*. She looked away again. Lorenzo's companion in the front passenger seat, turned his head and looked but seemed to find nothing amiss.

She waited a minute or more before glancing down again and selecting Jim's name. A blank message pane opened. She looked away. She waited. She typed: h – e – l – p. She looked away again. She waited. She typed: m – e.

She felt sure they'd noticed. Lorenzo's eyes were now fixed on her for as long as he could whilst returning attention to the road ahead. His partner was gesticulating, indicating that he'd seen or heard something.

Julia picked up the phone. There was no time to type anything more. She scrolled and selected *add attachment*, called up the image of *Leda and the Swan*, selected it and pressed *send*.

Lorenzo had pulled the car to an abrupt halt on the hard shoulder. His partner was out of the car. He opened the rear door, dragged Julia towards him and wrenched the phone from her hand.

"Stupid bitch." He threw the phone to the ground and stamped on it repeatedly. "That's a sure way to get yourself killed." He cuffed her across the face. She fell back and felt her head jar as it collided with the back of the driver's seat. The door slammed behind her.

He climbed back into the front seat and the car moved away again at speed.

Julia picked herself up, resumed her seat and said nothing.

The two men began arguing. Why hadn't Lorenzo searched her to remove the phone? Why had his partner destroyed the phone without finding out if a message had been sent? What good would it do either of them if Signor Lando got to know what had happened?

They argued on until they left the Autostrada at Vimodrone and headed for the outskirts of Milan.

The outcome, Julia thought, was that they would probably say nothing. They were too scared of getting into trouble with Lando. She'd got a message to Jim. The *Leda and the Swan* painting would tell him more than the few extra words she might have been able to add before the phone was taken away.

The main gates of a rundown factory complex opened as the limousine approached and they drove into a large warehouse building where there were half a dozen freight tankers and an assortment of smaller vehicles.

"Get out," Lorenzo said. His partner was holding the door open for her, waiting to see how she negotiated the task of getting out of the car in the short, short skirt. As she started to rise, he placed his hand between her thighs, caressing the soft skin at the top of her legs. She pushed him away and smiled. He gave her a lascivious look. "Maybe later tonight when you're not busy."

They took her to the far end of the warehouse, up a flight of stairs that she negotiated immodestly, to the amusement and delight of her captors following behind and they led her into a small office.

The two men spoke with deference to the distinguished-looking grey-haired man who sat behind the desk. "Signor Lando, I believe this is yours," Lorenzo said, offering her up as a gift to him.

Chapter 43

It didn't take Alfieri Lando long to realise that something unexpected was happening.

This woman was dressed like Emelia but clearly not her. In its own way as wonderful and exciting as it was of concern. How fortunate it had been that he'd been here in Milan taking personal control of the shipping arrangements. But then the gods that served him were often mysterious in the ways they took care of him. Some fate had brought her to him like this, and it was his duty to find out what this meant.

What had happened at the airport was already clear. A woman purporting to be Julia Blake had left Bergamo just under two hours ago on a flight to London. A woman purporting to be Emelia Rossellini had been detained by his men and brought here. The women had swapped identities. Sitting before him, dressed like a whore, was Julia Blake, the woman that his wife had allowed to investigate the family paintings.

He smiled.

He would alert his men in London about Emelia's arrival there. Even if they couldn't detain her at Heathrow, they would soon track her down, he was sure.

And now, he had Julia Blake. Except, she was not meant to be here. A check at Bergamo airport would reveal she'd left for London a little under two hours ago. No one but himself knew the English woman was in fact here. Lorenzo and his men hadn't understood what had happened. No one knew anything about this. Yes, his gods had provided well for him. He could do exactly as he wished; no one would be any the wiser.

He would keep up the pretence. "Now, Emelia, tell me what on earth you were doing in Bergamo?"

"One of my friends was leaving on a trip to Paris," Julia said.

Alfieri tried not to show any recognition that her Italian was appalling. "And who might that be?"

"One of the girls. Ursula. She has an important client there."

He admired her courage. There was no girl called Ursula. He knew that. "You should have asked permission. Zella or Matteo would have handled it."

Julia had no idea who Zella was but Matteo was the boyfriend Emelia had told her about. "There wasn't time. I only found out she was leaving an hour or so before she was due to set off. I know I did wrong, but perhaps you could forgive me."

It was all going so well, Alfieri knew it. "You know there are no exceptions. We expect and demand absolute loyalty."

"And I have always been loyal to you and the Lando family."

"Yes, Emelia, it's true. And so, we may be able to make an exception. Providing you do exactly as I say."

"I'll do anything, Signor. Anything to win back your trust."

222

"I'm going to need to move you away from here. Call it a period of rehabilitation."

"I'm not going back to Firenze?"

"Not until I am sure."

Julia was aware she was now in over her head. But to quell the real fear building inside her, she thought of Emelia, making her escape from this place, finding safety and meeting up with Jim.

"We'll go to one of my properties near here," Alfieri said. "Where you can relax and work through what caused this sudden lapse."

Julia smiled, and, as she imagined Emelia would have done, she fluttered those false eyelashes.

Alfieri was delighted. She would go willingly, unaware of what he had planned for her. He would drive her there himself. He would be the only one to know.

It was all so fitting. Leda had given birth to twins. And now his gods had sent him twins. There was a beauty and a symmetry in that.

Chapter 44

Matteo Lando was in turmoil. He'd killed a policeman. It had been sloppy. It was not like him.

Orletti had died before he could find out what he knew. He'd died in the back of Trentoni's van. The loss of blood from the stiletto wound too near the heart had finished him.

Dismissing Trentoni and using the van himself, Matteo had taken the body and sent it out on one of the waste consignments leaving from Milan. By now it would be on its way to somewhere in Africa. He didn't care where. But Orletti was a policeman and sooner rather than later the police would be out searching for him.

He looked up as Zella entered the room. She'd come to hand over the money the girls had brought in from the previous night's work. Matteo was silent as he counted each clip, logged it in the accounts book and placed it in the high security briefcase that he used to carry the money to Alfieri. He could tell Zella knew there was something on his mind.

He closed the case, locked up and approached her. He placed his arms around her in a long and secure embrace.

"I killed another man."

"Perhaps it was necessary."

"Orletti. A policeman. Snooping on our family. I didn't mean to kill. Just to hurt him to get him to talk."

"You cleaned up?"

"I did it myself. No one will suspect."

Knowing how remote Alessa was, Zella was sure she herself was the nearest thing Matteo had ever had to a mother. He brought her all his sinful acts, as a cat would bring dead birds to its owner, and she absolved him of them.

"I will have to kill another man. Alfieri will demand it."

"Who this time?"

"Trentoni, a decorator; he was there. He will not talk but Alfieri will want all possibilities covered."

"Don't worry about the killings. The life you have been born into is what is responsible. You are left with no choice, you have to live your life out as you find it."

He'd been offered the expected absolution and experienced a deep, sensual feeling of relief.

Chapter 45

The rush. Heroin.

How many times had he shot her full of the brown liquid, injected it into her helpless body?

Julia felt like some other person, an abstracted form of an earlier self, trapped in this existence.

As far as she could tell, he had her tied in a chair, bound at hands and feet. No pain from the cutting bonds. No pain of any kind; no worry, no stress in the midst of profound distress.

In front of her an object she'd once desired, one she had set her whole career on finding. The colours glowed with a super real intensity. This must have been what Dali and de Chirico and Ernst were striving for. The fluency that turned colour and reflected light into music.

Michelangelo's *Leda*.

It must be an apparition. How else could she be seeing it? Yet here it was, improbable, arresting, real, real, real.

A voice somewhere near, quickly approaching.

"Time to take you back to your room and get you ready for another shot."

Alfieri Lando would have to carry her out himself. But she was light enough and that was the way he wanted it. No one else must know what was in this secret place.

Julia could feel the bonds being untied but she was too weak to respond.

In another room, the sickening smell of the brown liquid being heated in the spoon.

"Jim, where are you? Can't you see your Julia needs you now more than ever?" But her words were lost.

Alfieri adjusted the mask and drew the cape around him. He peered out through the eye holes in the mask and admired himself in the mirror.

Yes, a god, no less. Something always meant to be.

He looked across to the red couch where his Leda lay, naked, her long hair untied now and falling over her apple breasts. That beautiful, euphoric smile worthy of Michelangelo.

As a god he had the right to take any mortal he wished and the mortal he wished for now lay there before him, consumed by the awe of his presence.

He moved slowly towards her to stand over her, parting her legs, enveloping them in the wings of the opening cape. He pressed forward and heard her whimper as he entered her.

Part Five

Florence, four days later
Wednesday September 3rd to Friday September 5th

Chapter 46

The sounds coming to me were those of an early-morning slaughter, what I first thought was a child being murdered but which, after a long period of uncertainty, I recognised as the wild shrieking of young pigs meeting their final end.

I had awoken in a sweat. The house at Monteverdi must be situated near a slaughterhouse, I thought. A normal business for people used to the countryside and its ways.

But this was not what had woken me. It was an unavoidable, nagging train of thought I couldn't dispel – the conviction that the reason why Lando's men had sought to attack us at the hotel was down to Miles and Sergio and their implicating of the Lando family in the illegal waste dumping. Miles had given the game away in the way he had so quickly understood the threat posed to him and those around him when he'd been told that Matteo Lando was involved with the murdered Emelia.

I dressed quickly and went down to the kitchen where I found Miles drinking from a large cup of coffee while Sergio looked on.

"It's the jet lag," Miles said.

"What time is it?" I asked.

"Some time just after dawn; around 6 AM. You couldn't sleep?"

"There's something I just can't put out of my mind. Thinking back to the escape from the hotel, just what made you so sure we would have to run for our lives?"

"You told me the Rossellini woman was one of Matteo's girls." Miles tried to make this sound matter-of-fact. "The photograph with Julia connected the woman to you. It wasn't difficult to see that the Landos would be coming after you."

"I don't buy it," I said. "They could have found me at any time. They weren't coming after me. There were coming after you. What have you done, Miles? Tell me."

"There are some things you don't need to know."

"About your investigation?"

"Yes, about the three years Sergio and myself have spent nailing the Landos for running what is probably the world's dirtiest waste dumping scam. It's not just the odd tonne or two of illegal industrial waste deposited in quarries in Italy and in the US, it's the thousands of tons of chemicals dumped in the rivers that provide the only source of water for some of the poorest in Africa. It's an environmental calamity that will take twenty years to clear up even if we stop it now. I want to see those bastards in the dock where they belong."

"That's all very well," I said, "but don't pretend the Landos were after me. You realised, didn't you, they could get to you just by knowing where I was. Now you are here in Florence with me."

"Here to help you," Miles said.

"It was hearing of Emelia's death that spooked you, wasn't it?"

"You need to trust me, Jim."

"Because you have my best interests at heart?"

"Because you shouldn't have been so deeply mixed up in this whole affair."

"I got 'mixed up' in this affair as you call it when a woman died in my arms in the apartment in London, a woman I was sure was my wife. You know that didn't give me a choice, Miles."

"And I've been doing my best to help."

"So, level with me."

Miles was silent, unable or unwilling to reply. Sergio shifted with unease. "You had better tell him, Miles, or I will."

When the words came, it was as if Miles was unburdening himself. "Sergio was approached by Giancarlo Orletti. He was undercover, investigating the family, seeking evidence that could put them away. We took him into our confidence on the illegal dumping investigation we'd been carrying out all these years. He thought it was the way the authorities might finally nail them. But we needed more hard evidence."

"And that's where Emelia came in?"

"Orletti had been grooming her as someone on the inside of the Lando operation who might be able to gather evidence for him. She had reason to hate them."

"So?"

"When I heard she had died there was a clear danger our operation had been compromised. And I was proved right. That foresight saved us all."

"From Alfieri Lando's men?"

Sergio interrupted. "Alfieri Lando. Or his wife, Alessa. She is the greater danger. It could have been her men who were sent to kill us."

The shrieking of the piglets in the nearby slaughterhouse rose to a crescendo and then abruptly stopped to leave a silence that I filled.

"It's always the investigation, isn't it? Nothing should be allowed to come between you and the result you've been working so hard to achieve. And I have to drag every last piece of information out of you as if it was your last breath. And if people get in the way…"

"Don't keep blaming us for Julia," Miles said.

"I need to know what happened to Orletti."

"The communication from Giancarlo stopped," Sergio said. "We haven't heard from him since I met him at San Berado."

I was becoming impatient with their failure to face up to the facts. "You and your investigation may have ended up getting Emelia killed, just as you imperilled Julia."

Miles frowned. "You don't know that."

Chapter 47

Travelling back along the A11 Autostrada that would take us back into Florence for the daily appointment with Inspector Manieri at the Questura, Miles was setting out the plan.

"The inspector is expecting you, but we've got to get you in and out of the Questura building as quietly as possible. We know the Landos have got someone on the inside there, and it won't be long before they're tipped off. So we have to get you in and out of Manieri's office quickly and undetected."

"As far as he is concerned, you are still staying at the Hotel Grande," Sergio said. He was driving the anonymous Opel, hired to replace the now-hidden pickup truck.

"OK," I said. "I get it."

I was smuggled into the Questura building after Sergio had pulled up the car as close as possible to the entrance. After the usual formalities with the desk sergeant, I was once more shown into Manieri's office.

"My daily report-in," I said.

"Of course," Manieri replied, as if, on being disturbed from some other more pressing task, he had just remembered why I was there. "Last night's pile up on the Autostrada. You wouldn't know anything about that?"

"Why would I?"

"I've been warned by Inspector Hendricks not to let you get away with avoiding answering my questions."

"OK. I don't know what happened. I hope the people involved weren't badly injured."

"Two of Lando's men are in hospital. One of them says he blames you."

"I was at the hotel all evening."

Manieri gave me a sceptical look. "In any case, it seems they will recover. Some broken bones and a great deal of injured pride, I hear. Speaking of Inspector Hendricks, he wanted me to let you know he and his team are still trying to de-encrypt the files that were left on your wife's computer. A difficult task. They have a team of four working round-the-clock to find the log-ins to all the files. Something to do with places in Cumbria, I believe."

"Where we spent our honeymoon," I said.

"He told me he suspects you of duplicity."

"I don't know what you're implying."

"You have a duplicate copy of the files and you must have de-encrypted them days ago. The information you discovered there is material relevant to this investigation and you chose not to reveal it. And you have come perilously close to perverting the course of this investigation."

I thought carefully before answering. I knew Manieri hadn't taken me into his confidence over the Italian police investigation into the Lando's affairs. I now knew there were informants sympathetic to the Landos in the Questura and that anything I confided to Manieri might find its way to them. But I reasoned that my best chance to continue my search for the truth about Julia lay in taking Manieri into my confidence.

"You're right, I have a copy of the files. They were given to me in London. Yes, I have de-encrypted them and I've spent the best part of the last two days reading through them, searching for clues to Julia's whereabouts. And, yes, that's where I got the picture of Julia and Emelia Rossellini that I showed you yesterday."

"And?"

I took out my phone, scrolled to select an image and showed it to Manieri. "There's also this." It was the shot of the two women with a handsome Italian man between them, embracing them both. "One of yours, I believe."

Manieri was surprised at what he was looking at. "What do you know about this?"

"I can tell you his name is Giancarlo Orletti. He's an undercover cop under your jurisdiction. And he's been investigating the Landos."

"Under conditions of the utmost secrecy, Mr Blake. This is really most concerning. You have a duty to tell me how you know this."

"I have to say, Inspector, you have been overwhelmingly considerate in listening to my requests about finding my wife, but give me the benefit of not considering me foolish." I cleared my throat and tried not to show my nervousness. "Your investigation of the Landos – it's the reason why you've been putting me off over the abduction and why you've been going slow over Julia's disappearance, isn't it?"

"No matter whether you are right or not, I am not at liberty to discuss these matters with you."

"But the investigation is already compromised," I said. "The picture proves it. Giancarlo Orletti knows my wife. He also knows the murdered woman, Emelia Rossellini. And there's something else I need to tell you."

"And what is that?"

I paused. "My brother, Miles, is not going to like me for this."

I told Manieri what I knew about the investigation into the Landos concerning illegal dumping that Miles was carrying out. Manieri raised an eyebrow when I told him that Orletti had identified Emelia as a source of the information that might lead to the proof needed to implicate them.

"This is a very serious matter," Manieri said. "That your brother could seek to compromise a police operation for his own benefit through an unapproved arrangement with one of my officers, putting him at risk, is unforgivable."

"But don't you see, we have a motive for Emelia's murder in this? Someone was seeking to kill her before she divulged the information about the Landos that she'd found."

"It is a possibility."

"Isn't it clear that the murder of Emelia Rossellini in London and the disappearance of my wife may be connected with the investigation of the Landos? If we are to find Julia, isn't it imperative to talk to Officer Orletti?"

"Signor Blake, Giancarlo Orletti has not reported in for over a week. It may not be as remarkable as you may suppose. Giancarlo is undercover. He has license to not report if he feels the investigation merits it." Manieri looked at me intently. "Not that this is any real business of yours. Let me emphasise; you will not get involved. I must warn you – interfering with a police investigation is a serious offence in Italy."

"But if he is missing, that might be connected with Julia's disappearance. The same people could be holding them both."

"We have no evidence of that."

"Something must have happened to Julia. Have there been no reports of any bodies found in the Florence area?"

"None that would match a description of your wife."

I could feel the rush of fear that had accompanied my last question subsiding. "There is another connection between Julia and Giancarlo – the note from him to her found in the apartment in London. Have you received details of that from Hendricks?"

"The note talking of his love for her? Inspector Hendricks was slow in letting us know about it. But, yes, we now have a scanned copy of it. Before what you have just told me, I had not made the connection with Officer Orletti. We have too many Giancarlos in Italy."

"The note is what Hendricks takes to be evidence they were having an affair."

"I would immediately dismiss the idea that this is proof of a link of any kind between them," Manieri said. "From what we now know, the note is more likely to have been written to Emelia Rossellini, carried there by her after her trip from here to London."

Something I should have been able to deduce myself.

"And I am surprised at Inspector Hendricks not understanding our Italian ways," Manieri continued. "If you want cover for an arrangement of the kind you suggest existed between Officer Orletti and Emelia Rossellini, what better way than to paint it as an assignation? If the note is discovered, people could be easily led to believe this is just what any red blooded Italian male would want to be doing with an attractive woman."

"Or they could just have been lovers," I said.

I had not believed that Julia was being unfaithful to me, as Hendricks was so keen to suggest. But I was relieved nonetheless to hear Manieri say this.

Manieri again looked thoughtful. "Signor Blake, I am pleased you have told me what you know. Our understanding of each other will be the better for it. But there are still many problems in accepting the contention that the investigation into the Lando's affairs has anything to do with the murder of Emelia Rossellini in London."

"Help me find the truth," I said.

"Then co-operate fully with me," Manieri said. "Make the files that you have available to us. Give us the de-encryption codes."

I removed Julia's drive that all this time I'd been carrying in my jacket pocket and placed it on Manieri's desk. I had earlier backed up all the information on a pen drive I'd obtained from Sergio. "I've placed the de-encryption codes in a new file on the drive."

"Inspector Hendricks is still insisting you might be guilty. He gives the impression that all he needs is sufficient evidence and he will be asking me to arrest you." Manieri paused, choosing his words carefully. "If such a request is made, I would not be able to refuse to implement it. You'll be at the hotel if I need you?"

"Yes, at the hotel," I said.

Chapter 48

I asked Sergio to drop me at the Hotel Grande. Miles left to pick up a hire car he would use to take him to a meeting in Milan.

But I returned first to the Bargello to tell Anna Pini that Julia had not died in London. Anna had to be told. I couldn't leave her in a state of distress.

She was still working on the Donatello in the large upstairs gallery but stopped when I arrived. She was at first surprised, then relieved, then troubled again. "You mean she may still be alive?" A tear of joy ran down her face.

"That's my belief. I won't accept any other conclusion." I looked into her eyes. "I have to find her. Anything you can recall could be important."

"There is something. It didn't seem to be any point in telling you when Julia was no longer alive." She took a deep breath. "Alfieri Lando came to see me, here at the Bargello. He knew my name. He knew everything about my position here as a conservator, as if he had someone in the ministry run a check."

"Disconcerting."

"He wanted to know about Julia. He already knew she was a friend of mine. He wanted to know how long I had known her. What interests we shared. I found him threatening. I may have said too much. He asked about Julia's friends. I told him about you."

I tensed. "What did you say?"

"Just what I knew. What Julia had told me. You are a radio producer in London. You have a brother who is an investigative journalist."

I thought back to my abduction in Borgo Pinti, to the meeting with Alfieri Lando when he'd known so much about me. Anna had been the unwitting source of his information.

Anna continued. "I tried to tell Julia she would be making a mistake working with such people. I should have tried harder, I know now. But restoring the Donatello, it has drained so much of my energy."

"Don't worry. You are a good friend to Julia. What you have told me is very important."

I thanked her and left the gallery, checking all the time to see if I was being followed as I made my way back along Via Ghibellina to where Sergio had parked the car.

Chapter 49

Sergio dropped me at the Hotel Grande.

"After all," I said, "I'm still checked in and paying my bill, so they would be expecting to see me."

"Be very careful."

"I want to talk with Ridley," I said.

I had unfinished business with the man, signposted in so many of the messages on Julia's pocket drive.

Once inside, I went to my room. I ruffled the bedding and messed up the towels in the bathroom to make it look to the hotel staff that I'd spent the night there. I picked up the phone and asked for a line to Ridley's room.

"We need to meet," I said, after Ridley had picked up the phone. "I'll come to your room. 623, isn't it?"

"Of course, Jim. It would be a pleasure."

I hated the way he called me "Jim" like that when I hardly knew him. I hated the insincerity in the man's voice. "I'll be right up."

It was on the top floor of the hotel; a suite that made my room look like a closet. Ridley offered me a drink as we sat on the comfortable chairs grouped around a large flat screen TV, an area larger than the whole of a standard room in the hotel. Ridley on the sofa, me in the armchair facing him with views over Florence from the nearby panoramic window.

Ridley began amicably enough. "So, what do we need to talk about?"

"Well," I said, "What do you know about Alfieri Lando?"

He didn't show surprise. "As a matter of fact, Jim, they came to the hotel, two of his men. They wanted to know about Julia's work. Then they told me they were looking for you. I told them that as far as I knew you were in your room. They weren't convinced. They threatened me. I had no idea what they wanted."

"Don't take me for a fool, Ridley."

"Meaning?"

"Meaning you've known all along about Julia's interest in the Lando's paintings. In fact, you've been trying to find out about Julia's activities here in Florence since the very day she left London. I've read her emails; it's all there, how you tried to control her work here."

"You had no right to look at that information. Your wife worked for me and any correspondence or notes on the work she was doing is the property of the studio, which I own. This is already a police matter and I will waste no time in telling them what you've done. Beyond the invasion of privacy, you've been tampering with police evidence."

I could feel my anger rising. "I'm already so deeply involved with the police that this is not going to matter. A charge of invasion of privacy and tampering with police evidence is something I can live with. You're not going to wriggle out of what I know about your involvement that easily."

"My involvement, as you call it – I've done no more than I have a duty to do as her employer. As I told you when we first met, I am here to continue the work of the studio, complete Julia's work here. What you are referring to is merely preparation for that."

"I know," I said. "You can stop the pretence. I know about Julia's work here; Julia has been looking for the Michelangelo, the *Leda and the Swan*."

"And how do you know?" Ridley tensed. "How could you possibly know that?"

I thought about telling Ridley about the image of *Leda and the Swan* sent to my phone. But an altogether different series of thoughts was becoming unavoidable. I would get nowhere using reason and logic with a man like Ridley, a man used to a world where politeness and manners were the necessary conditions for his keeping what he had, as he wanted it.

I moved closer and looked more intensely into those self-admiring eyes.

"Why don't we just say you need to take my word for it."

"So what are you saying?"

"You knew all about Julia's involvement with the Landos because you were harassing her in all those emails, trying to force her to tell you about her activities all along. Trying to find out what she had found."

"You can't prove any of this."

"Oh, you've been careful, I grant you that. But here you are in Florence, snooping about, pretending to have the interests of the studio and the legacy of Julia's work at heart and all the time you haven't been able to wait to get your hands on what she discovered."

"You must be suffering after the death of your wife. It's the only way of explaining why you would want to propose such falsehoods."

I chose not to tell him that Julia didn't die in London, that she may still be alive.

Ridley sought to assert himself. "This meeting is over," he shouted. "I'll be in contact with Inspector Hendricks straight away. That's right. The inspector was very understanding when he interviewed me in London. He warned me about you. I don't know what kind of stunt you're trying to pull here, but I'll let him know just what you've been saying."

I'd passed the point where the feelings of anger that had been growing ever since I'd entered the room could be controlled. Ridley knew more, I was convinced of that. If I was ever to find Julia, I would have to discover what he was hiding from me. Beneath the anger was this steady, cold logic.

"The problem for you, Ridley, is I just don't have anything more to lose."

I moved quickly, pushing Ridley down on the sofa and placing the weight of my body on top of him, pinning him in position. Before he had time to protest, I had both hands on his neck, squeezing the life out of him. Because it had been so sudden, Ridley was rendered helpless. His legs thrashed but he was easily held in place as the lack of air in his lungs weakened him. His face reddened, then began to become bluish. His eyes bulged. I knew it would be easy to carry on and kill him.

I found myself wondering, as I looked out through the panoramic window at the Duomo, how many times in this town the life had been crushed out of men like Ridley.

I looked back down just in time. He would be dead in another thirty seconds. I might have killed him but for the rush of blood spurting from Ridley's nose; a red flag bringing me back to reality.

I removed my hands. They were covered in Ridley's blood. The blood soaked my shirt. Ridley was in danger of choking on the part of it that had entered his mouth. The man's face contorted as he struggled to get air into his aching lungs. I allowed just enough respite, ten deep breaths or so, before tightening my grip once more.

"Tell me what you've really been doing here in Florence," I said. "Tell me and tell me quickly or, swear to God, I'll kill you."

Ridley's eyes were pleading. I relaxed my grip.

At first the words would not come. There was a terrible, gasping struggle for air. But then, slowly and painfully, Ridley formed the words between his trembling blue lips.

"I have a contact inside the Lando camp. Someone to give me a line on what Julia was doing, what progress she'd made."

"And…?" I tightened my grip ever so slightly and could see immediately from the look in Ridley's eyes that this was enough to make him continue talking.

"She told me Julia had found the painting, the *Leda*, under one of the Lando's pictures."

"Who told you?"

"Zella. Zella DeFrancesco."

"And…?"

"She works for them, runs their business, runs their whores…"

I thought immediately of Emelia. DeFrancesco would be the one running her. I tightened my hands on Ridley's neck once more.

"That's all I can tell you," Ridley said. His eyes were pleading. "She told me Julia had been to the Lando house in Lucca and had scanned the pictures there and had found the *Leda*."

I tightened my hands once more. "And where is Julia?"

"I don't know. I swear. She's dead; she died in London."

Having pushed the man so close to death, I had no choice but to believe this was all he knew.

"Get me a meeting with DeFrancesco. Do it now!"

"Why would she agree to meet you?"

"Just tell her I have information about Emelia Rossellini."

"Emelia?"

"Just get the message to her."

"You'll have to release me."

I removed my hands, stood up and moved away from him, allowing Ridley to sit up, weak, coughing and heaving. I took a towel from the bathroom so Ridley could mop away some of the blood that now covered him. I washed his blood from my face, hands and arms. I gave him a look that made it clear I would finish him if he didn't cooperate.

"I can call her," he said.

"That and nothing else. And speak in English so I can hear what you're saying."

"The phone."

I picked up the room telephone and Ridley told me the number to dial. When it rang, I only then handed it to Ridley. He spoke quietly and directly, explaining the need for the meeting as I had instructed him.

"It's done," he said. "Three o'clock at the Guggenheim in Venice."

"OK," I said. "Don't think about the police. Go near them – tell them what happened here and I will let Alfieri Lando know you've been spying on his family with the help of DeFrancesco. I would think that would almost certainly be the end of both of you."

Ridley looked back apologetically. "Just go," he said. "Leave me."

I turned and walked to the door without a word.

So, it had come to this. I was back with Danny and June in Birmingham and the routine, unannounced violence that was part of every day. I felt the shame of what I'd just done, as I'd been made to feel the shame of hurting that kid at school. And I knew the years between when I'd played the game of being polite and mannered and educated where every conflict had been verbalised almost out of existence had counted for little. If I was to find Julia, there was no other way.

Chapter 50

Three hours later, as set up by Ridley, I met Zella DeFrancesco at the Peggy Guggenheim Museum in Venice. I was careful to make sure I hadn't been followed, taking the train to Venice and then the vaporetto to the landing station near the Academia, then the short walk along the network of lesser canals leading to Fondamenta Venier. There were enough twists and turns to make sure I could tell there was no one on my tail.

I found her looking at Max Ernst's *Attirement of the Bride*. I could see her attentive face clearly reflected in a mirror on the wall opposite. I took the chance to snap a photograph of her with the mobile phone before she knew I was there. As I approached and stood beside her, she didn't turn to look at me, but instead began to speak as just one tourist talking to another.

"The paint is so thick because he used a special technique to press it onto the surface and leave behind those wonderful textures."

"Yes," I said. "But why meet here? Why the Ernst?"

"I spend as much time as possible here. It sums up the fate of us all." She checked herself, coming out of a reverie and turned to face me. "The reason I agreed to the meeting, against my better instincts, is that Signor Ridley insisted. He told me you had important things to tell me about Emelia Rossellini."

"It's connected to the disappearance of my wife, Julia."

"I don't understand the connection."

"Emelia was found dead in London."

"I didn't know that."

"In my apartment."

She looked at me for the first time, sensing that more was to come.

"I held her as she died."

"How?"

"She'd been shot in the back of the head. Assassinated."

"And the connection to your wife?"

"I thought it was her." I noted Zella's look of puzzlement. "You see, she looked just like Julia. She was her twin."

Zella's hands began trembling, as if trying to control either an overwhelming sense of rage or the desire to break down in floods of tears; I couldn't tell which. "How could that be?" she asked. I realised then she'd never met Julia.

"They were unknown to each other, sent for adoption to different families. Julia to the Bates' in London. Emelia to the Rossellini's here in Italy."

"That can't be. Everyone knows Emelia was Rossellini through and through."

"The DNA evidence says otherwise. Emelia and Julia, the police tests showed their DNA is identical. They were identical twins. A single split egg."

Zella returned her stare to the Ernst painting. It showed a pregnant woman, breasts exposed, naked except for a long red taffeta robe that extended to cover her face, so you couldn't tell if she had the face of a woman or that of a bird. Beside her on her right stood a mutant bird with a man's legs that brandished a broken, pointed, phallic spear. To her left, a younger, more chaste version of herself, dressed only in a winged headpiece, looked on. Behind them lay a dream landscape borrowed from de Chirico.

"I couldn't work out the meaning," she said. "How it had such a hold on me. I thought it summed up my life up to now. But, after what you've said, I know all this time it's been telling me something quite different."

She was so affected that if I had not taken her by the arm, I thought she might have collapsed. "Emelia was an innocent. I would not have expected that. They must not have told her. The Rossellini's must have raised her as their daughter and not told anyone."

Zella fell silent. She must have been thinking of how she'd helped Matteo to ensnare Emelia and lead her into a life of addiction and prostitution. How she'd taken satisfaction in what she had done.

How she'd observed Alfieri Lando taking great pleasure that a member of the Rossellini family had been brought so low, how he'd raped Emelia and how much she loathed him for it but how she took satisfaction from Emelia's humiliation. How she'd sought to orchestrate the affairs of the Lando family to cause the greatest possible harm to that family as a whole. And how she was probably now no better than those she'd come to take vengeance on.

"Are you sure you are OK?"

"I'll be fine," Zella said. She continued staring intently at the painting before her. "It's the girl," she said at last. "She deserved none of this."

"So help me. Help me find Julia."

"Your problems are your own, you must know that."

"Can't you see that Julia's life depends on getting to her as quickly as possible?"

"I don't know where she is. That's an end to it."

"You told Ridley she'd found the *Leda*. Is it true?"

"It's what he wanted so much to believe."

She walked away, leaving me staring at the *Attirement of the Bride* and thinking just why its strangeness had affected her so much. She hadn't denied that Julia might be alive, telling me she didn't know where she was. I found a slender strand of optimism in that.

Chapter 51

The exit from the Peggy Guggenheim was at the rear, on one side of the Sculpture Garden. It took me once more out onto Fondamenta Venier, the narrow alleyway running along the back wall of the gallery complex and alongside a waterway where half a dozen speedboats were casually moored alongside the dwellings on the opposite bank.

I'd gone only a few yards when I realised I was being followed. A youngish man had left the museum just a few seconds after me and was walking a few paces behind me along Fondamenta Venier. I walked more quickly but the man behind matched my change of pace. It was only two minutes to the Academia Bridge and the vaporetto stop where I would be able to board the boat and be taken back to the train station. It was just a question of crossing the next canal at the Piscina de la Forner Bridge, heading straight along the narrow alleyway beside another canal and turning right to reach the Academia Gallery. But as I made my way along this twisting route, the man behind followed my every step.

As I rounded the Academia Gallery and looked over towards the vaporetto stop, I saw that, without much attempt at concealment, there was another man in the alleyway, cutting off the vaporetto escape route.

As I tried to turn sharp left and head off into the labyrinth of narrow alleyways and bridges that would have formed the perfect maze in which I would be almost impossible to find, I found my way again blocked at the first bridge crossing on one of these lesser waterways by a third man. He was younger than the thugs I'd encountered working for Alfieri Lando. As I approached him, he said, "Signor Blake, Matteo Lando would like to have a meeting with you."

The man fumbled with something in his jacket pocket, showing just enough of it to let me know it was a gun.

They escorted me over the Academia Bridge and into San Stefano Square, turning right to head off along the narrow passageway of Calle Zaguri. We walked in silence but as we neared a restaurant a few minutes' walk along this narrow street, the man who had challenged me at the bridge said simply, "We are here."

It was a small family run restaurant, closed now in the break between lunch and the forthcoming evening meals. A few locals were seated around an old-fashioned bar at the rear. The men who brought me here joined them, shaking hands and exchanging embraces. Except for the man with the gun, who sent me upstairs where there was a dining room with ten tables set out for dinner. The only means of escape would be back down the stairs and that was blocked by the man with the gun who remained there.

Matteo Lando was seated at a table near windows giving a view over the street, his face illuminated by a strong shaft of sunlight.

"We were going to kill you once Zella had lured you here and found out what you know," Matteo said without looking up. "A stiletto through the heart before you reached the first bridge as you left the Guggenheim. That was the plan. But what you said to Zella changed that."

I stood there, facing Matteo, trying to come to terms with the narrow margin with which I must have avoided disaster at the hands of a woman who had seemed so vulnerable and unthreatening and yet had deceived me completely.

"She phoned and I was able to call my men off in time," Matteo said. "Then she checked with one of our contacts in the Questura, and, yes, it is true what you said; Emelia is dead and she was not Rossellini after all."

A single tear formed in the corner of Matteo's eye. It began to run slowly down his right cheek and then stopped, glistening in the sunlight illuminating his face. I couldn't help thinking this was the first tear Matteo had ever shed.

"You really cared about Emelia," I said.

Matteo nodded.

"Yet you abused her. The Landos used her as a whore."

Matteo corrected me. "Made her into a whore. Because Alfieri demanded it. Because she was a Rossellini."

The tear ran on. It was not replaced by another.

Matteo told me how the Rossellinis had become the sworn enemies of the Landos. He told me about the turf war, the deaths, about how the Landos had banished the Rossellinis to the South. And he told me how he'd deliberately ensnared Emelia in Milan and brought her here to Florence.

"You and Zella," I said, "You drew her in and broke her down, all for revenge?"

"For Alfieri's revenge. For his pride in seeing the ruination of the Rossellinis and their kind."

"And why are you are now telling me this?"

"Signor Blake. Half an hour ago you were going to be a dead man. Now that everything has changed, I want you to know this."

"And my wife. Emelia's sister. You know where she is?"

"If I knew I would tell you. But it's too late for a man like me to help anyone. That's all I can say." His eyes glanced towards the stairs.

"You're saying I can go?"

He phoned the guard at the bottom of the stairs who came up immediately.

"Escort Signor Blake to the vaporetto," Matteo said. "Make sure he arrives safely in Florence."

I thought about Zella. Was she now using Matteo just as she'd used me?

They escorted me, as instructed, all the way back to Florence. They sat a few seats away on the vaporetto and in the same carriage on the journey from Venice station. But it was a dubious kind of protection at best. Being protected by Matteo's men when in all probability his father's men were still searching for me left only ambiguity and dread.

Chapter 52

As the train was pulling into Florence station, the mobile phone rang. The two men that Matteo had insisted should accompany me looked up. I would have to keep my voice down and keep it brief. It was Manieri. Would I come to the Questura?

Matteo's men interpreted their instructions literally, so once I'd left the train and walked out onto the station concourse, they melted away in the crowd. I waited a few minutes, pretending to be interested in a coffee at the stand, before heading out of the station and queuing for a taxi. Within a few minutes I was heading through the Florence streets towards the Questura.

Being shown to the Chief Inspector's office was becoming routine. But what greeted me was anything but what I expected.

"Mr Blake, how nice to see you." It was Hendricks.

"Come to arrest me?" I was trying to hide my surprise.

"Not this time. In any case, I wouldn't come all this way, just for that. I'd ask Inspector Manieri to do it for me."

Manieri smiled. "There is a new complaint against you, Mr Blake. A serious assault carried out by you at your hotel. We should be investigating you; it is a serious accusation."

So, Ridley had gone to the police despite my threat to make his activity with Zella DeFrancesco known to the Landos.

Manieri continued. "But Inspector Hendricks has something that occupies our attention more fully for the moment."

"Something unexpected," Hendricks said. "Something we nearly missed. Something my instincts as an unreformed copper of the old school turned up." He paused for effect.

I recalled that first time in Hendricks' office, when I'd been brought in thinking that Julia had died. Those too wide-set eyes, the shaved head, the still evident pattern baldness – nothing had changed the feeling that I would not trust him if he was the last man on the planet. Yet I had the pugnaciousness of this man to thank for the knowledge the Julia had not died in London.

"We found plenty of samples of DNA that matched your wife and of course yourself, Mr Blake," Hendricks went on. "You might say those samples and those easily achieved results coloured our perceptions. But many victims, if they are not paralysed by fear when they are attacked, instinctively reach out, claw at their attacker. My unglamorous police background told me that. I went back to the body and saw that one of the fingernails was chipped. So, I asked the forensics team to go back, to run a more thorough check. To take new DNA swabs from under the fingernails, using the new micro sampling method they have just brought in. And there it was, unmistakable. Traces of blood with a completely new DNA signature."

"You'll be telling me next you don't think I did it," I said. "Did you get a match?"

Hendricks shook his head. "That's where your spineless friends who oppose the UK police DNA database come in. No, Mr Blake, we didn't get a direct match. Until the database is more complete, we have to proceed by indirect means in many cases. We have to deduce the possibility of a match from other records."

"Inspector Hendricks has the distinction of being one of the first in the UK to bring a serious offender to justice by using the DNA records of a near relative," Manieri said. "A rapist who attacked more than thirty women. His sister's DNA was on record from when she was taken in on a drink driving offence two years before, I believe."

"It was enough to complete the picture," Hendricks said. "We had interviewed the man several times but never made the connections we needed to allow us to see him as the monster that he was. The DNA result made those connections. We put him away for twenty years. And you know something, Mr Blake; the man's sister was never charged with any drink driving offence. Her body alcohol was within the legal limit by the time we tested her."

"The new DNA," I asked. "The sample you got from Emelia's fingernails, do you have a distant match?"

"I thought you might be interested in that," Hendricks said. "In fact we do. And that's why I'm here. The match is rather distant. I doubt if it would stand up in court. A cousin, convicted and imprisoned for fraud. It points to someone who is here in Florence – Clinton Ridley."

"The reason I phoned you," Manieri began, "you may have evidence."

I leaned back in the chair and pulled up my sweatshirt to reveal the shirt beneath.

The bloodstains were still there.

The attack on Ridley at the hotel had left me feeling angry that I'd resorted to violence, and in another minute I might have killed the man, and that no good would come of it. The meeting in Venice with Zella DeFrancesco had nearly cost my life. Those were brute facts.

But what had saved Ridley could now be the man's downfall. The rush of blood from his nose that had jogged me back into focus had drenched my hands and spattered my shirt. My hands had been covered in Ridley's blood. I'd washed my hands in Ridley's hotel bathroom. I'd not had time to clean the shirt. My thoughts had been to get to Venice in time for the meeting with Zella DeFrancesco.

I was aware of the irony. Some good might come of the attack on Ridley after all. Yet the rage that had led to the attack had come from part of myself I thought I'd mastered and, like a recidivist gambler who had scooped the pot on his first return to the table, winning, not losing, was the worst of my fears.

Chapter 53

When I again met Sergio for the planned return to
Monteverdi, I could see he was concerned. He listened in
silence as I told him what had happened in Venice and in
the meeting with Hendricks and Manieri at the Questura.

"You know this is dangerous," he said finally. "Yet you
get lured to a meeting, far away in Venice, telling no one,
going there alone. Just what did you expect?"

"There wasn't time to take you into my confidence. I
have to find Julia."

"But you can't go on taking such risks. It will be of no
help to anyone if you get yourself killed."

"I touched a nerve – with Matteo Lando. He was
unable to accept that Emelia Rossellini couldn't have
been born into the Rossellini family. It mattered to him.
That's the only reason why I was allowed to escape. It got
beneath his skin. It saved my life."

"Then all the more reason to take care, to work with
us in the way we have learned to work the Lando story."

"I don't have three years. I don't even have three days.
If they have Julia somewhere, every hour counts. I have
to take risks, don't you see that?"

Sergio remained silent.

"I need to know about Giancarlo Orletti. What links
you've had with him."

"He was told I was involved in investigating the illegal waste shipments and he demanded a meeting. I agreed to meet him at San Berado. He made me tell him about the shipment from Milan. And he must have sat on the information. There was no one there but me when those trucks came running out of the industrial complex in North Milan carrying that filthy stuff. I was well hidden. I was able to take a few pictures, but they don't mean much – pictures of trucks leaving a large warehouse facility heading somewhere, anywhere. I was unable to follow. It was too dangerous. They've probably moved the stuff halfway across the world by now. And not a policeman in sight."

"What about the warehouse?"

"It's an anonymous building, owned by the Landos. I guess they were collecting the waste there, before shipping it out. That's where Miles has gone; to check it out. But there's unlikely to be much that's incriminating at the place. The paperwork is kept by Alessa Lando. She heads up what they try to pass off as the legitimate part of the business."

"Nothing to point to where Julia might be?"

"Nothing."

He could see I was tired and dispirited. "There's something else."

"I nearly killed a man, Sergio. I lost it. I became someone I never thought I'd be again."

"We're dealing with people for whom violence is an everyday fact of life. The Landos don't think twice."

"We have to be better than them."

"No, we have to beat them."

"And then?"

"Stop worrying about the morality of this. That's a sure way to get yourself killed."

Sergio remained tense. He was sure we would be attracting too much attention, coming and going from the safe house like this. It wouldn't take much, a stray report from one of the villagers to the Landos, and our cover would be blown. "Too much risk," he said. "Going back to the house directly from the Questura, all the more chance of being followed and losing our security there."

We left the Autostrada and completed the journey in silence.

When we arrived, I went straight upstairs to the shower. Ridley's blood had caked my chest and stomach and had been baked-on in the heat of the day. Its smell was overpowering. I was not leading a normal life, I knew that. But as the water from the shower played over my body and I rubbed on the soap, I was convinced the stench of the man would never leave me.

The night passed fitfully and I was no nearer to finding Julia.

Chapter 54

Zella knew Matteo was drawing close to the state of mind she'd been engineering for him for so long. He needed one more push, one more dilemma to make the final step.

"Matteo, there is something I need to tell you about Alfieri. I've thought long and hard about whether I should tell you this, but I'm sure this is something you have a right to know."

He said nothing and stood there, waiting.

"You've heard about Emelia?"

Matteo spoke the words slowly. "Not a Rossellini."

"No, an orphan. Adopted."

"We should have known."

"Alfieri knew," Zella said. "I looked over some old papers of the family. He is on the board of the charity that supports the Carpasian Order. They were the ones fronting the adoption. Emelia's birth parents, killed by a bomb in Ireland. Alfieri arranged the adoption, for the baby to go to the Rossellinis."

"As part of his revenge?"

"As a way of increasing their punishment. Offering Rossellini's wife a measure of hope when she'd lost so much, planning to snatch that hope away when the time is right."

"And he used you and me to accomplish it, to bring Emelia Rossellini down."

Zella nodded. It was all that needed to be said about that now.

Matteo knew now what the problem was. It was not the killing of Orletti. He'd killed before, many times. That was not what was worrying him. It was what they'd done to Emelia. What they'd made him do to Emelia. A life ruined as revenge for an indiscretion of her family in the past would be understandable, but, as he'd learned from the Englishman and now from Zella, she'd deserved none of this.

It had been his responsibility to corrupt her. And he'd shown her no mercy; even though she'd told him she loved him. That was what was burning into his soul like a hot wire through ice.

Chapter 55

I arrived early at the Questura. Instead of being led to Manieri's office, they showed me to a darkened room on the second floor. It had a one-way mirror that looked into an interview room. Sitting on one side of the table, biding his time, was Hendricks. The two chairs opposite were unoccupied. Hendricks had all the appearance of a hunter waiting to ensnare his prey.

"It is a special arrangement," Manieri whispered. "Under a reciprocal agreement with the UK, I have permission from the State Prosecutor to allow Inspector Hendricks to carry out the interrogation. The crime was committed in London. The suspect's main language is English; it makes sense."

"And Ridley?"

"He's with his lawyer, preparing for the interview." Manieri paused and adopted a more conspiratorial tone. "I have to emphasise, Signor Blake, that your being here is a strictly off-the-record arrangement. The hope is that when you hear Ridley's account, you may gain some additional insight into the fate of your wife. It is a special favour, an arrangement you must keep secret."

"I understand, and I'm grateful," I said.

The door to the interview room next door opened. Ridley walked in with his lawyer, a large man, Herbert Santoni, an Anglo Italian with a reputation for gaining acquittals in cases where the defendant had little hope. Ridley had chosen well and had been wise enough to refuse to answer any questions until his lawyer was present.

Seating the two men, Hendricks turned on the video recorder and spoke into the microphone. "Interview with Clinton Ridley, commencing at 9.00 hours on Friday, September 4th."

Santoni gave a reassuring smile to his client. "I am Herbert Santoni and I'm a lawyer representing my client Signor Clinton Ridley. I'm sure, Inspector Hendricks, that you will ask only appropriate questions concerning the allegations against my client and you will respect the right for him to take advice from me not to answer those questions that might prejudice him in the future."

"Of course," Hendricks said. "However, I would advise your client to be open and truthful; it will serve him best. Officially, I have to caution your client that anything he might say can be used as evidence against him."

Ridley nodded.

"Now, Mr Ridley, where were you on the afternoon of Friday August 29th?"

Santoni tapped Ridley's arm, a signal that he should answer the question. "I was here in Florence on that day," Ridley said.

"And you didn't travel to London?"

Santoni tapped again. "I told you, I was here in Florence."

"I have here," Hendricks said, "a printed record from the airline authorities at Bergamo airport. It shows that a passenger listed as Clinton Ridley departed on a flight at 11:00 hours for London Heathrow. Can you deny you went to London?"

Ridley was unfazed, but Santoni showed surprise. He didn't tap. "My client reserves the right not to answer."

"Then let me ask you this," Hendricks said, "were you aware that Julia Blake departed on the same flight?"

"My client reserves the right not to answer the question," Santoni said.

"But you don't deny you knew Julia Blake?"

Santoni tapped. "Of course not," Ridley said. "She worked for me, in the restoration studio that I own and run. Of course I knew her."

"And you don't deny that your relationship with her, over the work she was doing, had become argumentative?"

"You are implying a state of conflict between my client and Mrs Blake that could be detrimental to my client's future interests," Santoni cut in. "He cannot be advised to answer the question."

"It's more than an implication," Hendricks said. "We have the email record of correspondence between Mr Ridley and Mrs Blake, retrieved from her computer hard drive in London. Those messages show a pattern of increased suspicion and anger over the work that Mrs Blake was carrying out here in Florence."

Ridley couldn't control himself. He answered before he could receive any instruction from Santoni. "The studio was founded on my reputation. Much of the expertise Julia Blake acquired came from me and my colleagues. She came to Florence on studio business but all the time searching for a masterpiece and making it clear what she found she would keep to herself. Don't you think that as her employer I had the right to be suspicious, and yes, to show a little anger at what she was doing?"

"I would advise saying no more on this matter," Santoni said.

"So you deny being in London on that day and visiting the apartment of James and Julia Blake on the South Bank?"

"My client reserves the right not to answer the question, Inspector," Santoni said again.

"We can play this game all day," Hendricks said. "But I have to tell you we have positive proof not only that you were in London but that you did visit the apartment in which a brutal killing took place."

"I have to request that you tell me the nature of the evidence you claim against my client," Santoni said.

"It's DNA evidence, recovered from the apartment. It's a perfect match with Mr Ridley."

"I have to tell you," Santoni said, "that if any of the alleged evidence was acquired improperly, it would not be admissible. My client has no DNA record in any database. How did you achieve a match?"

Hendricks smiled. "The sample was obtained as part of another investigation, one in fact that your client initiated."

Ridley paled. "The complaint I raised against James Blake for attacking me at the hotel?"

"Yes that's right, Mr Ridley. James Blake was required to provide any evidence in his possession of the attack he had made upon you. Your blood stained his shirt. The shirt was taken as evidence. The DNA from the blood on the shirt matched the DNA recovered from the apartment in London where the killing took place. It was discovered beneath the fingernails of the victim."

Santoni lowered his head. "I need to request a five-minute break, Inspector, to talk with my client."

Hendricks spoke into the microphone. "Pausing the interview with Clinton Ridley at 9:20 AM."

Looking in through the one-way mirror, I watched as Ridley and his lawyer left the room. "What now?"

"Santoni is a professional," Manieri said. "He knows that what Ridley must have told him before the interview was a pack of lies. He'll be telling Ridley he should not have tried to deceive him. He's likely to be suggesting that given the weight of the evidence against him, he should come clean in the hope of a lesser sentence. But knowing Santoni he might have a more elliptical strategy. We have to wait and see."

There was not long to wait. Within three minutes Ridley and Santoni were back in the room. Hendricks spoke into the microphone. "Resuming the interview with Clinton Ridley at 9:25 AM. Sit down, Mr Ridley. Do you have anything more to say?"

It was Santoni who spoke first. "My client apologises. He has decided to tell you the truth, in the expectation that it will be taken note of that he co-operated fully with the enquiry and that this will be taken into account in any action brought against him."

Hendricks said, "Of course. Then, I have to caution your client again that anything he might say can be used as evidence against him."

Santoni nodded.

Ridley remained silent for much longer than those in the interview room or those watching and listening from the adjacent room expected. It was as if he was making a final calculation. Was this the only course of action open to him? A fly in a web; was it really the case that the more he chose to resist the worse it would become for him?

At last he spoke. "Yes, I went to Bergamo airport. Yes, I boarded the same flight as Julia Blake. She didn't know I was on the plane. I was first off at Heathrow, it was easy to avoid her there."

"So you followed her to the apartment?" Hendricks asked.

"No, it wasn't necessary. I knew where James and Julia Blake lived."

"So why did you follow her to London?"

"You are right about the painting. She'd found it. The masterpiece. Michelangelo's *Leda and the Swan*. Beneath one of the paintings in Alessa Lando's collection. She found it and would be famous, and she was not going to recognise me. I was never going to allow it, you must understand?"

"So how did you know she'd discovered the painting?"

"I had it from someone inside the Lando operation."

"And do you want to tell me who that was?"

"Zella. Zella DeFrancesco."

"She convinced you to go to London?"

"Yes. She told me Julia had gone there to make a deal of some sort with a newspaper, to set up some arrangement whereby she would announce to the world she'd found the picture and was going to restore it. I had to make her see sense, that she couldn't do this without reference to me. Imagine the ignominy I would face, being cast aside like that, not acknowledged when one the greatest masterpieces was rediscovered."

"The gun. Where did you get the gun?"

"After I landed at Heathrow I went straight to my office at the studio in Mayfair. I kept the gun in my desk drawer, for extra protection. I just wanted some extra bargaining power. I never intended to use it, just to threaten Julia, to make her see sense."

"The bullets?"

"I bought them to defend myself. Dum-dum bullets. My army. If you are going to use a gun."

Hendricks suppressed his anger. "But you did use the gun."

"I went to the apartment. It was easy to get in. When I got to the Blakes' door, I pretended to be James, that I'd lost my key. I was let in. When Julia saw me she immediately overreacted, telling me to go away. I grabbed her; I told her she had to see sense. I took out the gun; made her face away from me, face the wall, with the barrel of the gun at the back of her head. I was telling her to be quiet. To listen to what I had to say, but she wouldn't listen. She started to scream. She tried to turn and reach back with her hand and she scratched my face. It happened. Some added pressure on the trigger, a response to the scream and the scratch. The gun went off, ripping into the base of her skull. She slumped, and there was blood, and I ran."

"The gun. What did you do with the gun?"

"I threw it in the Thames. It sank way down, no one saw me."

"I have to tell you, Mr Ridley, that the woman you killed was not Julia Blake. And I have to tell you I am charging you with the murder of Emelia Rossellini in London on the afternoon of August 29th."

275

Once he'd heard this, Santoni raised a hand. "My client will be pleading not guilty to murder. It was an accident. He had no intention of killing Julia Blake. He had everything to gain from keeping her alive, the knowledge she had about the painting was what Mr Ridley wanted. He had no motive for wanting to kill her. But you must explain why the charge is raised for the killing of Emelia Rossellini rather than of Julia Blake."

Hendricks turned to Ridley. "You didn't know Julia Blake had a sister, and it was the sister who was there in the apartment that day?" Ridley shook his head.

Santoni smiled. "Without a clear motive, Inspector, your case for a charge of murder will be difficult to bring. I ask you to consider the lesser charge of accidental killing. My client has been open with you. He has admitted he made a terrible mistake."

Hendricks didn't reply. He spoke into the microphone. "Concluding the interview with Clinton Ridley at 9:45 AM."

Two uniformed officers entered and took Ridley away to the Questura cells, followed by Santoni.

Hendricks was fuming. He turned towards the mirror and shouted, "Ridley pointed the gun at the back of Emelia Rossellini's head, pulled the trigger and she died. That's murder." He stormed from the room, no doubt to finalise the details of the charges.

Chapter 56

In the viewing room, Manieri turned to me. "There is the cleverness of Santoni. He already has his defence in place. Accidental killing. Ridley could be out in four years. He'll exploit the fact that Ridley thought the woman in the apartment was Julia Blake and thus had no motive for killing her. On the contrary, he had every reason not to kill her if he wanted to find out about the painting."

"By putting a gun to the back of her head?"

"Unwise, threatening, but perhaps not murder when the gun goes off. But to come to the point. Did you hear anything that might be of help in the search for Signora Blake?"

"Two things, First, just what a despicable piece of work Ridley is."

Manieri nodded. "And?"

"Zella. Zella DeFrancesco. I've met her. In Venice. She nearly got me killed. She's close to Matteo Lando."

I told Manieri what had happened in Venice. "They were shocked, I could tell, when they heard it was Emelia Rossellini who had died in London instead of my wife. The fact that her DNA matched that of Julia really threw them."

"DeFrancesco?"

"No, both of them. Matteo Lando was the most affected. He told me that before he knew of this, they'd planned to have me killed. Once he knew, the plan changed. It saved my life. Once again, it comes back to the Landos."

"It doesn't help," Manieri said. "Just about everything bad here is blamed on the Landos. They use that and men like Santoni to shrug off any and all such accusations. We would need real, reliable proof."

"Tell me about Matteo Lando."

"He's been suspected of many things, murder among them. But he is a shadowy figure. Few would admit to having even met him, let alone offer to give evidence against him."

"And DeFrancesco?"

Manieri logged into the computer at the workstation in the room, "DeFrancesco… There's no record of anyone of that name in our database." He called up more pages. "And there's no record of anyone of that name in the Interpol database either."

"Yet Ridley, if he's telling the truth, says she told him about Julia's flight to London."

"We only have Ridley's word for it. He could have been contacted by anyone. Made the arrangements himself."

"I know she's deeply involved with the Lando operation."

Manieri upturned his palms. "Without evidence."

"So we're getting nowhere." I could feel depression descending once again.

"There is something more I need to tell you, Signor Blake. Officer Orletti is now officially regarded as missing.

He is one of ours. We intend to find him, or find his killer if indeed he has been killed in action. We will be locking down this town, with every available man out there, seeking to find him. This may mean that other cases such as yours are set to receive a lower priority. I can only apologise, but I want to be honest and truthful with you."

So, nothing had really changed. Emelia's killer was now known but in the search for Julia it seemed I was no further forward. And I had a new fear. With Manieri locking down the town to find Orletti, it would be even harder to get any information on where Julia might be.

Chapter 57

I convinced Sergio of the merit of the drive to Bergamo. The idea was we could also check out the industry complex in North Milan where Sergio had witnessed the exit of the waste-carrying trucks. We would meet Miles who had gone there to investigate. I didn't tell him this was my way of doing something, anything, to try to dispel the gloom that Julia was out there suffering and the task of finding her was becoming more not less difficult.

Soon we were making progress, speeding along the Autostrada out of Florence. Outside the afternoon sun was fiercely interrogating the parched Tuscan countryside. In here, the air conditioning gave us a false removal from the heat of the day.

My job was as lookout for signs that we were being followed.

I tried to imagine Julia travelling the same road, heading to the airport with Emelia. It was the way it would have happened, I was sure. It would have been the easiest way to manage the identity swap under the pretext that it was Julia who was leaving. But then I came to an important question that surprised me that so far that it wasn't one I had thought to ask.

"Why did Emelia need to get out of Florence?"

Sergio was startled by the suddenness of the question. After all, we'd been travelling without a word for almost fifteen minutes. "What caused that to pop out?"

"What was so important that Emelia needed to leave Florence as she did? What would have convinced Julia to give up her identity to her, to make such a large change of plan?"

"They were close, they were twin sisters. They would have had the kind of bond that meant they would do anything to protect each other."

"Yet they had only known each other for little over twenty-four hours. You would have thought they would have done anything to stay together, to have more time to get to know each other."

"Unless there was something of such magnitude that Emelia just had to leave, right then."

"Enough to make them risk being apart. Emelia's life was already the kind of nightmare any woman would want to escape from. A life of drugs and prostitution, being run by Matteo Lando. Yet she'd stayed through it all, out of loyalty to Matteo, even love for him, so Manieri told me. Something worse, far worse than that, otherwise she would have stayed and Julia would have found a way to take her out of the life here, in her own time."

I pulled up the picture of *Leda and the Swan* on my phone. Her last message to me, sending this and calling for help. I thought it was about the painting, but maybe it was about something else entirely. I stared at the picture, the brute force of the beast about to rape the innocent, at the dazed euphoria of the young girl's face and in that moment I knew. And with that knowledge came a new horror that bit into my soul: if Julia had taken Emelia's place it was she who was now in danger of a dark depravity.

In another twenty minutes, we arrived at the airport. A flock of tourists was pouring out of the terminal exits, surprised to find they'd arrived not, as expected, in Milan but thirty miles away in Bergamo – a place airline logic called Milan (Bergamo).

We were parked nearby and watched as it dawned on the visitors they would need transport and began to queue in the heat at the taxi rank.

I tried to imagine what would have happened when Julia had emerged from the terminal after seeing Emelia off on her flight to London.

"She would have been dressed as Emelia and attempting to look as much like her to allow her sister more time to escape," I said.

Sergio nodded. "They – the Landos – have a reputation for being ruthless with any of the women they run who try to escape. Just leaving Florence for no good reason would have risked a beating or worse."

"So how did they arrive?"

"Taxi is the most likely. It would have been too dangerous to have taken a lift with anyone that Emelia knew in Florence."

"Then, Julia would have left by taxi again." I looked at the long queue and the small number of taxis that were servicing them. "This is the kind of town where there is no more than a couple of dozen cabs."

I pulled out my phone again, selected the picture of Julia, Emelia and Giancarlo smiling in the restaurant that I'd discovered in Julia's files and pressed, "zoom". I centred the enlarged image on Emelia's face. "If Julia had dressed herself up to look anything like Emelia, then this is what she would have looked like. We have a likeness to show the drivers."

I looked back at the taxi rank. All the taxis had gone with the first passengers to arrive. A line of over fifty tourists remained.

There was nothing to do but to wait until the taxis returned and the tourists departed. That would take some time. We decided to go into the airport building and wait.

Sergio went to the self-service for coffee and returned with two espressos in the smallest of paper cups.

"The three guys over there." He gestured towards a group of men who had gone to sit at a table on the opposite side of the cafe. "They work on the taxis. Must be on a break. I could hear them talking about their fares, which of the women passengers they fancied. We could try them."

I handed Sergio the phone. "You do it. You might be able to get through to them."

Sergio went over and spoke with the men but he was soon back. "They hardly looked at it. They were completely uninterested."

We waited until the lines of tourists outside had cleared and the taxis had returned to wait for the next batch of arrivals. The response was the same – a hostile lack of interest.

I didn't know what I'd expected to find. One of the drivers, perhaps, who would give a lead on where Julia had gone after she left the airport dressed as Emelia. But we were going to get nothing here. I felt demoralised as we returned to Sergio's car and headed back towards the Autostrada for the journey to the north of Milan.

We headed for the large warehouse that Sergio had staked out three days before when the Landos were moving the latest of their consignments of illegal waste. We stopped at the meeting point we had agreed with Miles – a rest stop off the main road.

Miles shouted through the open window of his car. "Anything at Bergamo?" Our silence told him more than we could have said.

There was no need for subterfuge as our two cars approached the warehouse complex. It was clear the place was deserted, a symptom of the lock down that had followed Manieri's drive to find Orletti. Miles told us he'd broken the lock on the gate easily with a crowbar from the boot of his car. He showed us that within the complex, everything had been removed. There were no vehicles, no signs of life. The main warehouse building itself stood empty. We had reached a dead end. Any hope of finding information leading to Julia or the fate of the illegal waste had been lost. "They've cleaned the place out expertly," Miles said.

Miles told us his deputy editor was arriving the next day for an early morning meeting with him in Milan and it would be best to book into a hotel for a fresh start the next morning. Sergio said we would be all right.

The drive back to Florence took place in silence between Sergio and myself. I'd stopped looking for signs that we were being tailed. I almost hoped the Landos would come after us; at least that might offer some way out of the depression that was closing in on me. Manieri was concentrating all of his efforts on finding Orletti's killer. The search for Julia was sinking to a lower priority with each passing hour.

We were approaching Florence. "Drop me at Hotel Grande," I said.

"Have you lost your mind?"

"I'm still staying there."

"They'll know you're there."

"I don't care. Let them come; at least I'll get some chance to get at the truth."

"I'll check in with you."

"No, go back to Monteverdi. I need some time alone. Time to think."

"Time to get yourself killed."

Sergio protested all the way to the underground hotel car park but I would not change my mind. He left for Monteverdi, agreeing to take a different route to minimise the chances of being tailed.

I lay on the bed in the room trying to focus on what I knew that would allow me to find Julia. I was sure she was alive, that she was in a desperate situation and that every hour counted and yet, here I was, alone and dispirited with no clear plan of how to find her.

A half-recalled image played in my mind. As Sergio pulled out of the underground car park, had a car started following him? I could not be sure.

Sleep descended before I had the chance to take off my clothes and get into the bed.

Chapter 58

In the still-hot night, a shimmering haze hung over the Arno. Lit by a full moon and the lamplight of the nearby streets, a swarm of mosquitoes buzzed in, hungry for prey. With an alien consciousness they hovered briefly over the floating mass but turned and flew away. No blood to be had here.

The body bobbled a little as it was prodded from under-water by something seeking a different kind of sustenance.

A young couple embraced each other and kissed in the moonlight. The boy looked down towards the water, unsure what he was seeing.

He told her to look where his eyes had taken him, pointing with an outstretched finger. Her expression changed. She had to agree it was a human body, floating in the Arno. Their romantic moment was forever blemished.

When the police were called they summoned a small boat. In full view of a growing crowd of spectators they removed the body, covered it with a tarpaulin and sped off.

Chapter 59

The phone rang. I rolled over and checked the bedside clock: 3:30 AM.

It was Manieri. He was sending a car to take me to the Questura. I had to be ready in five minutes. I put on my clothes and made it down to reception to be greeted by a plainclothes officer who flashed a badge without giving me time to inspect it.

"Tell me what this is about?"

"Inspector Manieri will tell you everything when we arrive at the station."

He drove in silence through the now-deserted streets taking me into the Questura building and up to Manieri's office without ceremony.

Manieri looked more serious than I had ever seen him. "We have a body."

My heart stopped. "Julia?"

"A man. Mid-twenties. Dumped in the Arno."

The relief that it was not Julia was short-lived.

"No attempt to conceal the body," Manieri continued. "A signal, a message. A ritual killing. Taken from behind with a garrotte; a gangster's assassination. A warning to others not to ask questions."

I could tell there was more to come.

"Signor Blake, I believe you knew him – Sergio Romani."

I couldn't hide my shock. "When?"

"Tonight. The body had been in the water no more than a few hours."

"There is no doubt?"

Manieri shook his head. "His fingerprints were easily traceable. Nothing had been done to prevent us from checking them."

"Sergio had a record?"

"A student activist, protester, troublemaker; we had his prints on file."

Sergio dead. I'd been with him just a few hours before. If I hadn't insisted on the fruitless trip to Bergamo, he might still be here. Had I taken more seriously the image of the car following him from the underground car park, I might have been able to prevent this. "You knew all along he was helping me to find Julia?"

"We are not so lacking in surveillance that we are unaware he was bringing you here to the Questura. It's all there on our video records."

I thought of Sergio's fears about an informer inside the Questura. His wish not to be seen was justified. And I'd exposed him.

"There is something else that's important, Signor Blake. We were about to question him concerning the disappearance of Officer Orletti. A priest at San Berado saw him talking with Sergio Romani there in the church grounds. As far as all our enquiries can tell this was the last time Officer Orletti can be placed before his disappearance. Now before we can interview Romani, he is found dead."

"And Orletti?"

"We are assuming that he, too, may have been killed."

Manieri looked into my eyes. "Signor Blake, the reason for bringing you here at this hour. I need you to tell me everything you know about Sergio Romani."

"I'm not sure I'm up to this. It's difficult not to think this is my fault."

"A natural feeling."

"He told me he was concerned about being killed. I convinced him to go on."

"He's gone. You must concentrate, Signor Blake. For the memory of your friend, for Orletti, for your wife."

"The Landos."

"Evidence. We must have evidence."

I nodded.

I took Manieri through everything I could recall that involved Sergio, from our first meeting in the hotel through to the last trip to Bergamo. I told him about the safe house in Monteverdi and about his work with Miles investigating the Landos in the illegal dumping story, about the tip-off he'd been given about the removal of the illegal waste from Milan and how Sergio had been disappointed that Officer Orletti had not reported it as planned.

"The purpose, then, of the meeting at San Berado a week ago?" Manieri asked.

"Yes, at San Berado."

"You should have told me earlier. Things may have been different."

"He was also told you have an informant here and we couldn't let these things be known in the Questura because the Landos would be informed."

Manieri frowned. "Another very serious accusation."

"It is something I needed to tell you. A reason why we couldn't be frank with you. A reason why I am finding it difficult to tell you this now."

"This woman, Zella DeFrancesco. You mentioned her last time we spoke. You know we have been unable to find her, or any record referring to her. We have no image of such a woman. We have been assuming she could be an invention of Ridley's and you have somehow been deceived."

"I have this," I said. I pulled up the image of Zella I'd taken on the phone without her knowing when I'd first met her at the Venice Guggenheim. I handed the phone to Manieri.

Manieri gazed intently at it for over a minute. "DeFrancesco? It is not her name. But I know the face. One of my first cases as an inspector. She certainly wasn't called DeFrancesco back then."

He went over to a large bank of filing cabinets that filled one wall of the office. He started leafing through the case files stored there until he found the one the wanted. "I keep a record of all my cases, even the ones from before we went digital. Personal vanity, no doubt, but useful." He opened the file and showed me the picture clipped to the front page. "Andrea Bellini. That was her name."

It was Zella DeFrancesco looking ten years younger. Yet the hard, intense look in her eyes was already there.

"A woman who has been through much," Manieri said. "I recall the details of the case very well."

He leaned back in his chair and told me what had happened those ten years earlier. Andrea Bellini's husband and her two sons had been innocent victims when they'd been caught in crossfire in a gun battle between the Lando and Rossellini families in the turf war that had cost so many lives. Her husband had been driving the children to school; the burst of gunfire had killed him outright and when the vehicle crashed it had gone up in flames. Her children had perished long before the emergency services could arrive.

"She lost her whole family. After the counselling, I assumed she must have gone away to mourn."

"You never caught the killers?"

"Two of the gunmen likely to have been involved died a few days later. We had no direct evidence against the Landos or the Rossellinis, though we knew of their war and tried to stop it. It was all we could do to prevent more innocents being killed."

"Leaving Andrea Bellini to find her own route to justice."

"Perhaps, Signor Blake. It has been a long day and a long night. We will return you to the hotel. I will arrange police protection. Find your brother. Get him to also go to the hotel. I can guarantee your safety there and only there. Await my instructions."

I left wondering how I could break the news of Sergio's death to Miles.

Chapter 60

Miles came in from Milan when I called him and told him I had to see him at the hotel. There was something important I couldn't tell him on the phone. He arrived just after dawn. I talked him past the armed and uniformed officer who now controlled the corridor outside my room.

"Something's happened," Miles said as soon as he passed the police protection.

I ushered him inside the room and closed the door. "Miles, I don't know how I can tell you this. Sergio's gone."

"Gone?"

"They've killed him. I was with Manieri half the night. It's a positive identification. Fingerprints. There's no doubt."

Miles' legs shook. He collapsed into the chair near the bed, heartbroken. "He was lecturing you to stop taking chances, to play by his rules and now this has happened."

"How long were you together as colleagues?"

"More than eight years. We broke some great stories."

"And close friends."

"More than that."

"I didn't know."

"That's the way we wanted it."

I put my arm around Miles' shoulders. "There's nothing I can say to make this any better. I just want you to know I don't feel angry any more about Julia being involved by you and Sergio in the Lando story. I was wrong to sound off like that."

"When did you see him last? I thought you were both going back down to Monteverdi."

"A mistake. One of the worst mistakes of my life, Miles. The last time I saw him he was heading back towards Monteverdi. One of them found a way of tracking him and killing him."

"How?"

"Miles, you don't need to know that."

"I need to know."

"It won't help."

"Tell me."

I took a deep breath and tightened my grip on his shoulders. "A gangster killing by garrotte. They dumped him in the Arno. As a warning."

Miles' grief was turning rapidly to hate. I could feel his body tensing, preparing to fight. "Anything. I'll do anything. Anything to bring them down. I don't care about the story anymore."

"You'll get the story. A tribute to Sergio. But first I need to know more about Zella DeFrancesco." I told him what Manieri had told me about her. "Can you use your journalism contacts, discover more about what happened to her?" I was doing no more than what he'd done for me back in London when he'd helped me through the shock of the news of Julia's death. Keeping him occupied. If Miles did suspect my motives, he didn't show it.

"Yes," he said, "I'll get onto it."

Chapter 61

When Miles had left to get all the information he could from his contacts, I picked up the phone and dialled the number I'd extracted from Ridley. Zella DeFrancesco agreed to meet when I called her "Andrea".

I recalled what happened last time in Venice when she seemed so fragile and yet had deceived me and nearly got me killed.

"Where can we meet?" I asked. "Somewhere here in Florence?"

Zella replied, "Too dangerous. You English are so recognisable here. Take the 9.05 train to Lucca. Sit in the first carriage. I will find you on the train."

It was already 9.00 AM. That gave me less than five minutes to get to the station. I managed it with less than a minute to spare. There was no time to buy a ticket; the lines at the ticket office were too long.

I found a seat in the first carriage as Zella had instructed but there was no sign of her. The train pulled out and I was left with my thoughts and the view from the carriage window.

The view changed as we approached and stopped at Montale Agliana, the first station beyond the old city. Looking down from the elevated railway line, I could see into the poverty-strewn streets, disfigured by graffiti, in which the dispossessed lived so close to the affluence of Florence itself. Across from the station, at the rear of a five-story block of apartments, was a display of washing hanging from the narrow balconies to dry in the sun.

I glanced back from the window and Zella was there sitting next to me.

"Montale Agliana. Where most of the girls live. I'm often out here with them."

I shifted in my seat. "Andrea, I know what happened to your husband and children. I know what you've being doing, getting ready after all this time to take revenge on those that killed them."

She was unfazed. "I knew someone like you would come along. I have been waiting for this moment. What do you want?"

"That something good should come out of this. A way of finding my wife, Julia Blake."

"Why would I trust you?"

"Because I know enough to convince Alfieri Lando that you have been plotting against him and his family all these years."

"A threat?"

"No, not a threat. An inducement to collaborate. To see we have a common cause."

"To bring the Landos down?"

"And to find Julia."

"To break the Lando curse."

"Why me? Why not go to Manieri?"

"The Landos have a plant in the Questura. Lambini. In Squadra Mobile. If I try to involve Manieri directly, Alfieri Lando is sure to be told. I will be dead in minutes. It has to be you, and you need to do exactly as I say."

She told me what she expected me to do.

The train pulled into the next stop. She stood and glanced at the bag she'd left on the seat. "You will need to use that. Just switch it on when the time comes." Then she was gone without a backward glance.

I got off at the next station, crossed to the opposite platform and waited for the return train to Florence. There was a seat at the far end of the platform where I could be alone. I phoned Manieri. He'd given me his direct number so there was no problem in negotiating with his receptionist.

"Signor Blake?"

"I need to meet you. Somewhere secure, somewhere private."

"Come to the Questura."

"No, not there. At Florence railway station. In the cafe by the ticket hall."

"Crowded. Noisy."

"A place where we would not be noticed."

"Signor Blake. So mysterious."

"I'll be there in twenty minutes. Tell no one in the Questura where you are going."

"And the reason I should come?"

"To find Officer Orletti's killer."

He closed the line. I could only assume he'd agreed to the meeting.

Chapter 62

The cafe near the ticket hall was as noisy as Manieri had said. When he appeared, he was alone, as requested. He came over and sat down opposite me. "Well, Signor Blake, I have shown my faith in you. I hope you will be able to repay it."

"Trust me, and do exactly as I say, and we can find Orletti's killer tonight."

He gave me a long look. "It is more normal for people, including even you I believe, to be doing what I say. This is hardly usual."

"Are you getting anywhere with the Orletti case?"

"There are some leads, but nothing definite."

"And nothing on Julia. Inspector, we need a break-through, something that gets beneath the secrecy that has fallen on this town since it became known you are searching for a police killer."

"And you are serious?"

"I've never been more serious in my life. What do you have to lose? One night. If you are disappointed, arrest me for impeding the investigation."

I could see he was weighing the options. "OK, Signor Blake, say I believe you, say I will go along with you. What do you expect me to do?"

"Phone the Questura. Send Lambini out on an assignment. It doesn't matter what it is. Just send him out of the building, out of town."

"Lambini?"

"He is informing for the Landos. You can deal with him later."

"And then?"

"Once Lambini is out of the way, we're going to need three of your most trusted officers, only those you can completely rely on. Out of uniform, armed."

"And?"

"Send them to the hotel at 7 PM. To the underground car park."

"Then where will we be taking them?"

"I'll tell you that when they arrive."

"Signor Blake, I have no idea why I should be trusting you like this." He smiled. "But it seems that trust you I must."

Chapter 63

We met the officers in the car park as arranged at 7 PM. Manieri came with two young male policemen, Giletti and Raimondi and a young female officer, Vanin. It was only once we were inside the unmarked car that I told them where we were going: San Berado.

It was little more than a ten-minute drive up the precipitous hillside leading to the church. The late afternoon light was not yet fading and the heat of the day remained as persistent as ever. The view over mediaeval Florence was remarkable, but I had no inclination to take it in.

We parked at a distance and walked up steep steps to the broad stone apron at the front of the church. Vanin was dispatched to take care of the old priest who patrolled the grounds. Zella had told me there was a possibility he was part of the Lando informer network. She also told me there would be two Lando men inside the graveyard at the rear of the church and that it was essential to pick these up before they could sound any warning.

Giletti and Raimondi disabled the first of them just outside the gateway that led to the graveyard. He was relaxing, taking a smoke break, and they quickly surrounded him, overpowered him and secured his hands with plastic snap-on bonds.

The second lookout was patrolling at a discreet distance from the Lando tomb but nevertheless keeping a careful watch on it. It was more difficult to ensure he would be captured without raising the alarm. Manieri and I stayed back while the two young officers circled round the rear of the graveyard, squeezing between the crowded, elaborate headstones and statues that had been erected above them. They were soon positioned close, waiting for the second guard to move closer towards them but he remained still.

"Surely he will feel the need to move soon," Manieri whispered as we looked on from our vantage point.

We waited. Then, after a few minutes, he began to walk towards the tombstone, a seraphic angel that Giletti and Raimondi were hiding behind. When he strayed close enough to them, they pounced, bringing him down quickly, disabling him, binding his hands and muffling his mouth. We had the graveyard under our control.

I produced the bag that Zella DeFrancesco had given me on the train journey. It contained a laptop computer with a Bluetooth receiver inserted in one of the USB slots. I powered it up and opened up the recording software. There was silence from the computer's speakers.

"We are out of range," I whispered. "We need to move closer."

As we reached the metal lattice door of the Lando tomb, the signal became clearer and we could hear voices being relayed from inside. Zella was wearing a wire. She was there with Matteo, somewhere inside the tomb.

Manieri started to express surprise but he was silenced immediately by what we were hearing.

Chapter 64

Zella stood in the corner of the largest room in the inner sanctum. Alfieri Lando sat in a high-backed red velvet chair that resembled a throne. On an easel to his right, proudly displayed, stood Michelangelo's *Leda and the Swan*.

Alfieri was angrily confronting his son, Matteo. "You know you are not allowed here. Why are you here?" He turned to look at Zella. "And you, what are you doing bringing him here?"

They were fully fifty feet underground in one of the many chambers burrowed deep into the hillside beneath the Lando tomb. Zella had told me that over many years they'd excavated into the rear of the hillside outside the church grounds under cover of supposedly legitimate building projects, constructing an array of chambers and passageways that were made to connect to the tomb inside the churchyard. The rear entrance now sealed up, the only way into the sanctum was through the tomb itself. Beyond the first few chambers in which the dead of the Lando family lay there was a farther passageway leading to the larger chambers below. The workers on those earlier building projects had all died or been killed.

Matteo shivered. Everything about this place chilled him. "We need to talk. You have been absorbed in your own world. So I found you here."

"What is it?"

"I have done what you wish. I have been a loyal son. I have killed for you more times than you can recall. Though you did not ask for it, I killed Orletti, the under-cover cop, snooping into our business. And you act now like I have betrayed you."

Alfieri burned with anger. "A bad mistake. Killing a policeman. Placing the family in danger."

"I have covered our tracks. I took the body to the warehouse in Milan myself. It was in bags, black rubbish bags. It went in with the industrial waste. Nobody there would have known what it was."

Alfieri would think hard and long about how to punish his son, but that would come later. "Your mistake will cost the family millions."

"My mistake? Tell me about Emelia Rossellini. About what you made me do to her."

"She deserved it. For what her father tried to do. To destroy this family. Do you think we should show mercy to any Rossellini offspring?"

"You don't get it, do you? Emelia was no Rossellini."

"I assure you, my son, I did not know that."

"I know. I know you are lying. You have known all along about Emelia." Matteo looked towards Zella. She nodded.

She'd found out about the secrets beneath the Lando tomb from the decorator, Trentoni. He knew what Alfieri would have planned for him once he'd been implicated as a possible witness in the killing of Orletti. He'd come to Zella and offered to show her what he had discovered while working on the tomb – the secret passageway that led to the chambers below – in return for her helping him to avoid being killed.

"The future of the family, Matteo. Don't you see you've placed it in danger with the killing of Orletti?"

"Don't you see, Father, that you have not been able to make me in your image. Though you have tried. A part of me still cares. I'm not hollowed out and heartless as you want me to be. As you are. I think that's what worries you more than anything. You don't care about Orletti or Emelia and all the others, you just can't face the fact that I'm not going to be like you."

"Maybe it is good you feel like that, like I once felt. It is to be expected. It means you are almost ready."

"Ready for what?"

"Ready to take your true place in the history of this family."

"That won't happen." Matteo turned to face the Michelangelo. He could see it clearly now. The woman lying prone was Emelia. The monster towering over her was his father. He attacked the painting with the knife he drew from a trouser pocket, slashing the painting with two long diagonal cuts that ripped through the surface paint and dug deeply into the wood beneath.

Alfieri tried to rise from the chair but Matteo hit him hard across the face and he fell down. "Son, Matteo, don't do this. This is all for you, for the future."

"I don't care to become like you. To become you, don't you understand?"

He slashed again and again at the painting, scouring the paint off its surface, smashing into the wood beneath.

Alfieri rose again, reaching for a gun he had hidden in the drawer of the table beside him. Matteo drew a stiletto, rushed forward and struck it deep into Alfieri's heart. He tried to reach the gun but the strength was leaving him. He slumped, blood pouring from his chest, convulsions wracking his body.

Matteo returned to the painting, slashing it, splintering the wood foundation into fragments, crushing it under his feet until he had all but destroyed it.

He watched as his father died.

He turned to Zella, walked slowly towards her and held her. "I killed a man."

"Don't worry, Matteo. You did what had to be done." She kissed him on the forehead, absolving him. He became limp, childlike.

They made their way back through the passageways towards the surface, past the long dead of the Lando family, trying not to inhale the perfume of decay.

–

We had heard everything that had been said since our arrival. The evidence sat now on the hard drive of the computer.

"I owe you an apology, Signor Blake," Manieri said.

We were waiting as they arrived at the entrance. Matteo was easily overpowered. He did not resist.

"Matteo Lando," Manieri began. "I arrest you for the murders of Officer Giancarlo Orletti and of Alfieri Lando. Anything you say may be used in evidence. You have the right to request a lawyer."

Zella led me back into the tomb while Manieri stayed to await the reinforcements that he'd called. We walked through the official part of the tomb with its marked stone caskets dating back hundreds of years.

When we reached the first large chamber via the secret passageway that Zella had led us through, I found Alfieri Lando dead. The pool of blood around him formed a dark stain.

Zella spat on his body. "It is what he deserved, for the harm that he has done to me and my family. This way I bring down not only Alfieri Lando but also his son Matteo. And soon I will bring down the whole family."

There was the sound of another voice coming from outside the chamber. I looked and found another door. I opened it and walked through into a second chamber. There was Julia, lying curled in a foetal position on a red couch, delirious, calling in the weakest of weak voices.

"Help me."

I held her in my arms. "Julia, my love, it's OK. It's OK. I've finally found you."

Epilogue

Eighteen months later

I drove the car up the gravel drive of the large house in Sussex where Julia had been in treatment since our return from Italy. They had cured the heroin addiction in six months but it was the counselling to overcome the trauma of the events that had taken so much longer. When her therapists thought the time was right, I had to tell her that her sister, whom she'd known for such a short time, had died at the hands of Ridley. It set her back. It was her attempt to save her that had led to her sister's death. It was still not clear whether she would ever fully come to terms with that. But today I was here to take her home.

Manieri had been keeping me informed about what had happened in Italy. Zella DeFrancesco was living in Switzerland with a new identity under witness protection after turning state's evidence and bargaining for no charges against herself in return for bringing down the Lando family. She'd placed herself expertly to implicate them all. When the Italian police raided Alessa Lando's mansion at Lucca on Zella's instructions they found details of shipments and records of payment relating to the illegal dumping of waste in Africa and South America. Alessa Lando was awaiting trial and expected to be given an eight-year sentence.

Matteo Lando received a thirty-year sentence for the murders of Sergio Romani and Giancarlo Orletti and a concurrent twenty-year sentence for the murder of his father. Giancarlo's body was never found.

A further eighty members of the Lando family were in the process of being convicted on Zella's evidence. She'd found a way of bringing the whole family down and gaining revenge for the death of her husband and children ten years before.

Hendricks was satisfied when he was able to extradite Ridley to London, put him on trial and see him receive an eighteen-year sentence for the murder of Emelia Rossellini.

Miles was able to file an exclusive on the illegal waste-dumping story in memory of Sergio and Orletti. Manieri put a twenty-four hour embargo on any information being revealed while Miles broke the story to the world's press.

Julia never found her masterpiece. The Michelangelo had been destroyed beyond repair even by the most skilled teams of restorers. Careful analysis of the remains of the picture by expert conservationists concluded that though the work was old it was likely to be a copy of the same quality and provenance as the copy in the National Museum. Michelangelo's original was in all probability still out there or had been destroyed long ago. The edifice that Alfieri Lando had built upon the family's long-term possession of the painting was, like everything else in his life, a fabrication.

But I didn't want to think about any of that now. I had found my Leda, and she was about to be returned to me.

Acknowledgements

I would like to express my thanks to Kath Middleton for her help and to many other friends for their kind observations and encouragement.

James Blake Thrillers

Take No More
Regret No More
Forgive No More